"… an inventive science parable that challenges conventional views of reality."
—Kirkus Reviews

Regina's Imagination Universe

Also by Joram Piatigorsky

Jellyfish Have Eyes Series
Jellyfish Have Eyes
Roger's Thought-Particles
Regina's Imagination Universe

Short Story Collections
The Open Door, and Other Tales of Love and Yearning

Non-Fiction
The Speed of Dark, a Memoir
Truth and Fantasy, Essays
Gene Sharing and Evolution, the Diversity of Protein Functions

Regina's Imagination Universe

A novel
by
JORAM PIATIGORSKY

TRUTH&FANTASY
MEDIA

REGINA'S IMAGINATION UNIVERSE

A novel
By Joram Piatigorsky

This second edition published in 2025 by Truth & Fantasy Media

For any information, please address Truth & Fantasy Media at books@truthandfantasymedia.com

ISBN: 978-1-964428-04-8
eBook ISBN: 978-1-964428-05-5

Printed in the United States of America

"I am a poor listener ... my drifting mind is a frustrating handicap, and makes me wonder, just what world do I inhabit?"

—Joram Piatigorsky,
Truth and Fantasy

Chapter 1

THE PRINCETON SENIORS received their college diplomas in alphabetical order, so Regina Resin would follow Jim Radloff, a classmate who was destined to take over his family's vineyard in California when his father retired. It was a no-brainer for him; he would fit into his family mold with the distinction of being the first owner of the vineyard in four generations to have a college degree. Regina envied the simplicity of deciding his future.

When Jim was called, Regina looked at her family in the audience. She was next. Her father nodded in response while he wiped the sweat off his forehead with the back of his hand. She focused on her grandfather, Roger Resin—Grandpa—beside her father, hoping the heat and humidity weren't too much for him. He had traveled from Elizabethtown, a hamlet in the Adirondacks in upstate New York, where he had lived for the last thirty years of retirement. She had urged him to come to her graduation despite being worried that at ninety, the trip might have been a bit too much for him. He locked his eyes on her and had his wide smile, so she assumed he was okay. He had said that he would be there unless he were dead. Yes, *dead*. That's what he had said: "If I'm not there, I'm probably dead." It was like him to speak of dying to emphasize that he was still alive.

When Regina heard his voice now in her mind saying only death would keep him from her graduation, she assumed the riddle was that he was afraid of imminent death, not that he had any worrisome signs of failing health. Death always wins, she thought. No one lives forever. But Grandpa? She had loved and needed him ever since she was five. He was her treasured support system—her grandfather, father, and mother combined—her whole family in one aging person. She was closer to him than to her parents or anyone else.

He had celebrated his ninetieth birthday a few months earlier at a dinner with a couple of long-term friends, both widowers, like him. Robin, his wife, had a fatal stroke a year ago, which had struck as suddenly and unexpectedly as lightning strikes its target. She had been his guiding light and inspiration for sixty years of marriage. Most of his other friends had passed away, leaving Regina, his granddaughter, his only solace. She gave him comfort and a vicarious future for as long as his health lasted. As for her, life without Grandpa was unimaginable.

Regina hadn't thought she would be emotional at this pivotal junction in her life, but now her knees trembled and her heart pumped an extra beat or two as she walked up to the stage to receive her diploma. She felt squeezed between reality and previous thoughts of graduation, which she had imagined as crossing the line from child to adult, dependent to independent. She would be twenty-one in a few months.

"Thank you," she said to the dean when he handed her the diploma. She smiled and waved to her family in the distance. She saw her life with no distinction between the order of things. She saw her mother in the crowd from the corner of her eye, smiling, as she often did, mask-like, as if injected with Botox. Mom, a model of mediocrity and a substitute teacher at the local school, was always there, neither for her nor against her. She seldom had an opinion of her own, and never had a contrasting point of view on any topic. Regina had often wondered whether her mother was bland by birth or was hiding behind a veneer. If reincarnated, Regina imagined her as a penguin following mindlessly the straight line of the birds ahead. \

Next to Mom was her father, poor Dad. When he had failed to become a senior partner in his Philadelphia law firm fifteen years earlier, he left the rat race seething with resentment. He escaped with his wife and five-year-old daughter, Regina, to Elizabethtown, and became a salesman at the hardware store. "So much for being a lawyer and its pathetic lifestyle," he had said. As Regina got older, she asked Dad on occasion why he didn't go back to being a lawyer. He reacted each time defensively and said that a salesman gave people what they needed at the time, just as lawyers did, but without the mess of the law. Mom often jumped in and said, "He's a good salesman, dear." It never varied.

These thoughts passed through her mind as she walked off the stage and tightened her grip on the diploma, which she viewed as her ticket to freedom from her joyless parents. Before sitting down, she glanced once more at Grandpa, who was trying to capture the moment with a camera. She turned her head away to avoid a photo in which her crooked front tooth might show; she often suppressed smiling to keep that tooth hidden. Although she was pleased, proud in fact, to be graduating, she hated the ridiculous tassel on her hat—so pretentious and in bad taste—and she felt uncomfortable in her graduation gown, which was too large and made her feel even smaller than her five-foot-two-inch, overly slim frame that made some people ask if she was anorexic. *That* she was not. Despite a hearty appetite and insatiable love of sweets, she stayed thin.

She didn't like looking identical to everyone else in her cap and gown; it made her feel like a formless pebble indistinguishable from all other pebbles. Regina was not like everyone else. She wanted Grandpa's photo to mark the birth of the real Regina, the special one, not just another student with a diploma, as she started her new journey after college.

But, she wondered, who was she? The one who seemed real to others or the one she imagined?

Chapter 2

AFTER THE FESTIVE graduation ceremony, Regina had an anticlimactic early dinner with her family in a charmless local restaurant. At least Grandpa toasted her in his warm style. Then they took the tiresome five-hour drive from Princeton, New Jersey, to Elizabethtown and arrived exhausted at two in the morning. After a brief sleep, Regina awoke at 7:30, had a banana, and waited an hour before calling Grandpa. It was a long hour for her since she was anxious to know how he had withstood the trip and what he really thought of the graduation. She had found it pompous. More importantly, rather than savor the moment, she worried about her future. She depended on him, as she always had, to give her good advice.

"Up and ready for you, Regina," he said, sounding sleepy when she called. Apparently, she had woken him up, so she waited an extra hour to give him a chance to take a shower and get dressed.

Regina, comfortable in jeans, sweatshirt, and sneakers, gave a rapid knock on the front door and bounded in without waiting for him to open it. She was carrying a paper bag filled with her favorite pastries, which she placed on the dinner table before turning to hug her grandfather. He was in his usual brown chinos, but still with his pajama top and bedroom slippers. She thought, correctly, that Grandpa would not have had much, if anything, for breakfast.

"Regina, help! You're strangling me!" he said, staggering to keep his balance when she threw her arms around him as if she hadn't seen him in years.

"Hang on there, Grandpa. Take a deep breath. I'm transferring Love-Particles to you. They're saying thanks again for coming. I was so happy that you did. I felt that we were graduating together, you and me, with degrees in science."

He had told her about Thought-Particles on several occasions, which he considered the highlight of his career. She loved the idea of Thought-Particles, literally thoughts as particles emanating from the brain that could randomly infect nearby individuals. What a brilliant idea, making us a combination of ourselves, our friends and colleagues, and others in the environment. She was proud to be the granddaughter of the distinguished and creative scientist she admired.

She recalled how often her presence seemed to transform him from a lonely old man to a loving grandfather. He smiled more and moved faster, almost with a bounce to his step. It made her feel like his daughter rather than his granddaughter, and made her comfortable to tell him everything, no matter how personal. She felt that he cared whether she was happy or sad or scared. He was her security blanket as she was growing up, providing the support and love she needed and craved, especially in her teenage years. Mom and Dad disillusioned her. They were good people, she knew that, but they focused entirely on what she did and who her friends were, the nuts and bolts of her life, not her feelings and conflicts.

When she tried to talk about herself, Dad usually yawned, and Mom occasionally said, "That's nice, dear," or "That's interesting," to show she was listening. They never asked about *her*. Why didn't she treat them as parents and tell them what she wanted to express? They would have to listen. No, she thought. It wouldn't work. People don't change that easily. Did they care about her, or were they only concerned with what she did, not what she felt? They didn't suffice as parents; her grandfather did, and her parents seemed happy to have Grandpa there for her. In that sense, he was a form of security for them too.

Now Grandpa looked tired, and she felt at fault for pressuring him to come to her graduation. His eyes were slightly bloodshot, he sagged a bit, and he seemed unsteady on his feet. Balance was a serious issue for him, as for most aging people, but it was getting worse. He had fallen a couple of times in the last month. Fortunately, he wasn't hurt, but it scared her.

"Forget it," he had said. "I tripped. It could happen to anyone."

"You're not anyone, Grandpa. Please be careful," she responded. "Maybe you should use a cane."

She knew he wouldn't do that. When she had suggested it before, he had always said the same thing, "Two legs are enough for me. Two legs, one head. That's it."

She typically answered, "I'm so lucky to have you, Grandpa. I need you here with me, not in the hospital." She wouldn't have dared say, "not dead." Even the thought felt like a pit in her stomach.

After a moment of silence, she looked straight at him and said, "Grandpa ..."

"Yeah, what?"

"I'm kind of mixed up about what to do. Most of my friends have applied to graduate school or have gotten a job for a year off from academics, or whatever. I haven't got a plan. I love science—you know that—but I also like to write. What should I do? Maybe I should become a writer rather than a scientist. Did you like the stories I sent you?"

"I love your stories, Regina."

"Really? Aren't they somewhat crazy?"

"When I read them, you become *Queen* Regina. There's a sense of royalty in your writing. You are a synthesizer of ideas. You are my Queen and think big, royal, inclusive. Crazy isn't always crazy. Sometimes it just sounds that way because it's ahead of the game. Maybe like Thought-Particles ... no, never mind. Who knows what crazy is?"

"I don't. That's for sure. And I don't know what to do now that I've finished college."

"A lot of people take a year off to think about their next step. Listen to your gut and be honest with yourself."

"I've never had trouble with my gut ..." she said, patted her stomach, and then paused.

Her mind retreated to her student days in high school when she had loved science above all subjects. Then she had graduated from

Princeton with honors in biology. The truth in science towered above everything else for her, a truth beautiful and perfect—uncontestable reality. No academic areas had definitive truths like science.

But she also loved to write stories, essays, biographies—just about anything that came to mind. She had won some prizes in high school for her short stories and had been editor of the *Daily Princetonian* in college. As for the subjectivity of literature in contrast to the objectivity of science, well, it gave her the challenge of expressing herself rather than being a messenger of nature. She loved the ambiguity of Joseph K's guilt in Kafka's *The Trial*. She hoped Grandpa, the smartest person she knew, could help resolve the jumble in her mind.

"Grandpa," she said, in a timid voice.

"Yes. What?"

"I never told you about what I did for my honors thesis in science because I thought you wouldn't approve. Anyway, it's no big deal. I guess, it reflected my conflict between science and writing."

"Don't keep me in suspense."

"I combined science with writing and made my honor's thesis in science a short story, very short!"

"What? How did you do that?"

"I don't know. I do crazy things sometimes."

"Tell me more."

"Rather than focusing on a specific area of science, I wrote a short story blending science with literature, sort of two for the price of one. I can send you an excerpt of the story from my phone now if you want. It's just a few lines. The whole story is a dozen pages of descriptions and questions a scientist might ask."

She emailed the excerpted story to Grandpa's computer.

A Lion's Universe, and I'm not Lying

A three-year-old African girl called Reggie was lost when she wandered at night from the safari she was on with her parents. Her despondent parents searched everywhere and one of the guides stayed with them searching for over a week, but never found little

Reggie. It broke their heart. She was discovered by chance years later by another safari when she was fifteen. She had been raised (so to speak) by lions in their wild, natural habitat. She had retained some human language skills from when she was three. Of course, she communicated best with her adopted family in "lion-speak," which combined diverse sounds—growls and squeaks with multiple variations in tempo, intensity, and intonations. Each sound carried different messages or thoughts. Lion-speak was about as foreign to humans as the rare click languages in some African countries. She was studied for years when she rejoined the human world and became invaluable for scientists to learn about the complexity and inner life of lions.

"That's all I have here. It's just a flavor."

Grandpa opened his eyes wide, furrowed his brow and scratched his thighs, a habit when he felt emotional.

"Grandpa ... are you okay?" Her left eyelid flickered a bit, which was her reaction when she was worried.

"Amazing, just amazing, Regina. So original and courageous and ... brilliant. My granddaughter. Queen Regina."

"Thanks," she said, unaccustomed to such praise.

After a moment of silence, she said, "The thesis was fiction, yet it wasn't. It was science, but not science fiction. The story transformed the world of lions into an entirely original universe. The last three pages—I can send you the whole story if you want when I get home. I dreamed up a bunch of questions that might be asked in the future, for example, do lions have aesthetic values or abstract thoughts or any conscious philosophy of life? The point was to look ahead. Well, I was also having fun! I didn't think they would really kick me out of Princeton in my last month."

"Send me the whole story. Congratulations from an old guy, who can hardly believe what you did."

"Hate to change the subject, Grandpa, but I'm hungry. Let's eat. Oh, I nearly forgot, the flowers," she said, and ran out to the car to rescue them.

Regina loved flowers, making spring her favorite season. She placed them in a vase she had given him for his eighty-eighth birthday, arranged the red roses and yellow tulips to make a pleasing combination, and placed the bouquet on the table.

"There. Looks great," she said.

"Smells good too," he said.

Regina had transformed Grandpa's house into a home in a few minutes.

She pulled up an antique Amish chair to the table to accompany the one that was there for him when he ate alone. She had a weakness for these chairs, which were relics from Grandpa's childhood. They were still sturdy, with the faded green and yellow paint adding an aged patina of authenticity.

There was relatively little furniture in the living/dining room combination—one soft sofa with cracked black leather upholstery, and two armchairs covered with soiled gray blankets. Regina had often wondered what the upholstery was like under the blankets but had never looked. There were lamps on the tables on each side of the sofa, but they didn't give enough light for him to read at night without straining. She had thought of giving him a miner's helmet with a light but never had. A coffee table in front of the sofa was covered with magazines, a book on black holes and another on art history. A Persian throw rug that hadn't been cleaned in at least fifty years lay on the floor in front of the sofa. He had his desk and computer, as well as shelves filled with books on many topics, and a TV, in his bedroom. His bed was unmade. It was a small house, good for an old widower like him. Yet Regina felt sad when she saw him try to keep the place in tip-top shape by himself, and she thought how lonely he must have been without Robin.

She went to get plates in the kitchen a few steps away getting ready for breakfast while Grandpa poured coffee into cups. She noticed him stacking dirty dishes and unwashed silverware in a corner under a towel to hide them from her. She set the table and placed a bowl of the fresh fruit she had picked up along with the pastries—chocolate croissants, apple strudel, cherry coffee cake, almond bear claws, a couple of glazed doughnuts, and four "everything" bagels. She didn't like the garlic, but she knew Grandpa did, so she bought them anyway.

Regina thought that someday she might write a short story about the table set for two with fruit and enough pastries for a midget army. She would imagine crooks planning a heist, or politicians running for office, or maybe mad scientists wondering about almost anything. Maybe they could be thinking about Thought-Particles, which Grandpa would like. She was always collecting ideas to write stories about. She had published one short story in high school about the thoughts of a young boy expelled from his classroom for continuing to talk when the teacher told him to be quiet. Her story was published in a local magazine and even promoted on the cover with a picture of a little boy, with a bubble from his mouth saying, "Imagination is truer than so-called reality." That was one of the proudest moments of her young life.

Satisfaction with the work was always her most important goal, but recognition was always welcome. Without it, she felt criticism, even if none was intended.

"So much food, Regina. How can we possibly eat all this?"

"We'll gulp it down, and you can save what we don't for another time. Got any peanut butter or jam for the bagels?"

He didn't. They ate, and then ate more.

"Regina, I can't figure out how you keep so trim with such a love of desserts. People who eat half as many sweets are overweight," said Grandpa. "You're a digestive phenomenon. Lucky girl."

She smiled, the heck with the crooked tooth.

"Here's my problem, Grandpa. I'm stuck between writing and science," she said, continuing what she had started before they ate. "And I don't know if I'm smart enough to do either of those two," she said. Then, with a softer voice, almost a whisper, but still audible, she added, as if to herself, but hoping Grandpa would hear too, "at least whether I'm smart enough to *really succeed* at them."

Defining "success" was troublesome for her. What exactly do I mean, she wondered?

Grandpa shook his head in disbelief. "Regina, come on. Not intelligent enough? You couldn't mean that. You're obsessed with understanding everything," he said, "not with talking for the sake of hearing your own voice, like so many who really aren't very intelligent at all."

"Really? Maybe, I guess. I close my eyes, which helps me imagine stories to write."

"See what I mean?" said Grandpa. "You're no dummy! You were telling me imaginative stories even before you could write. Remember how you would stay up late at night writing long after your mom and dad went to bed, and how you stapled the pages together in the morning and gave your 'book' a title? Oh my, how you loved to write fantasy and stories beyond belief which you called your 'crazies.' If anyone laughed, you asked them to define reality. Imagine, thinking about reality at such a young age! You're telling me that you're not smart enough? Your stories made me think about what's real and what's imagined and never failed to transport me to new worlds of wonder. You have a fierce imagination."

"Aren't you going a bit overboard, Grandpa? That's okay. Keep it up!"

"Happy to," he said.

"Remember how you identified with *Don Quixote* when you were twelve or thirteen? You read it three times!"

"How could I forget that?" she said. "I loved the gallant Don, and still do. Know the best part about him? It wasn't just his fantastic imagination; it was that he let his imagination become his true world. I love that guy. I don't have the courage to live out my imagination as he did."

"I'm kind of glad you don't. What books do you like now?"

She said that she found modern books focused too much on technology, artificial intelligence, and robots. "They're interesting for sure," she said. "But they're so technical. I think that makes them more about machines than humans. I still like my 'crazies' the best," she said, with a chuckle. "I like to imagine and make-believe as if they were real. Everything seems like an illusion today, and the programmed robots are treated as if they're alive, which they aren't. I like real people, flesh and blood humanity. I admit, however, that robots do challenge the notion of truth and life itself."

"That may be your problem, Regina. You could succeed in just about anything. You would be a great writer."

"But I do love science, a lot. It varies with my mood. What could be more important or amazing than life—evolution or how our brain works? Writing is limited to my imagination. On the other hand, there's no end to the imagination of nature. How does everything work—life, genes, the *ability* to think and imagine? I bet that brains will be programmable to function even better than nature made them someday. I can't wait until brain engineering blossoms into a scientific revolution," she said, her voice going up a notch higher. "Brains will become manageable, like computers, and able to regenerate when damaged, like the liver. Being demented or senile will become a problem of the past. I guess technology isn't that boring after all!

"Did you know that we're on the brink of being able to grow back missing limbs in people by activating the right genes in the right cells at the right place? It even turns out just some metabolic changes can promote regeneration. I read the other day that scientists can make adult frogs regenerate legs, and there are encouraging experimental results for monkeys being able to regenerate a leg. I predict that amputation will soon be simply an annoyance for a few weeks until the missing structure grows back. It's about reorienting enhancers and promoters, switching transcription factors, genetically engineering stem cells with a program, like Winthrop published last year, that ..."

She stopped.

What am I trying to prove? she thought. That I know more science than Grandpa?

Grandpa seemed to be listening and no doubt understood a lot, but Regina guessed that he must also be annoyed when she talked as if he knew everything about the science that had developed after he had retired. His eyes lost their usual gleam, and he scratched his thighs, as if they itched. She didn't see him do that when she talked to him by phone from Princeton, but he did become quiet when she went on and on about her science courses. When she thought she had spoken too quickly, she slowed down, but that didn't seem to change anything. When she asked him what he thought about certain things in contemporary science, he seemed to struggle to understand. She tried to explain, but he still seemed confused. Yet he always told her to continue, that he was happy she was learning so much. She assumed that he got the drift of much of what she said and continued, but slower, with few technical terms.

"I'm ninety," he admitted at times, and would say, "you're learning complicated things that I don't know anything about. But thanks for educating me."

That made her feel insensitive. Knowing less science than she, a college student, knew must have depressed and embarrassed him, an accomplished, lifelong scientist. Science and technology had advanced so much since he had retired that it must have sounded like magic to him now. Maybe he really was grateful to hear about science going on today.

She asked herself how much she knew about what he had done scientifically. He had mentioned his concept of Thought-Particles, so she knew about that, and he had told her about his mistake thinking he had identified a gene for imagination, but that was about it. She didn't understand exactly his concept of Thought-Particles or how they fit into science at the time. What mistake did he make when he thought he had identified a gene for imagination but had to retract his publication announcing it? He never gave her any details, and she had never asked. She was his granddaughter, not his colleague. His work was history, and how often do young scientists read about that? Not often.

"I know it's getting late, Grandpa, but can you give me a quick version of your highlights before I go?"

"A quick version?"

He raised his eyebrows but didn't respond immediately so she waited. What was his problem?

"Well," he started, "I got an unexpected call a couple of weeks ago from a journalist from the *Daily Gazette* in Bethesda, some newspaper I'd never heard of. I know this sounds strange, but she wanted to interview me. If you think your short stories are crazy, I think anyone wanting to interview *me* is crazy."

"An interview! That's exciting. You agreed, of course. Did the journalist say what she wanted?"

"I don't know where to start," he said.

"Don't worry. I'm interested in whatever you say."

"Maybe you can help me figure out what to do. You're not the only person with an imagination that can take over. Where do you think your Imagination genes come from? Mars?"

Regina was pleased to have him acknowledge her genetic connection to him.

"The interview. What exactly did the journalist say? How did she think you could help her? You've been retired for a long time, but then again, you're a famous scientist. She sounds smart and …"

"Slow down," he said.

He shook his head and said that the journalist's call had caught him by surprise. It was the last thing he had expected.

"I was almost ready to tell her that Dr. Resin is out of town and expected to return in two months."

Regina laughed. "I'm the writer here, not you."

He ignored her. "No, I didn't say that. I asked her why she wanted to interview me, an old guy who retired thirty years ago. 'I'm irrelevant at this point,' I said, and was prepared to hang up. Yet, she began to tell me what she was after, what her project was about."

Regina leaned forward. "What's the journalist's name?"

He scratched his thighs.

"Strange about that," he said. "She never told me her name. Her news organization publishes their articles as anonymous editorials. They thought that knowing the authors and their reputations would influence the reader's interpretation of the article. They wanted readers to be objective. Well, maybe. I don't know.

"The journalist wanted to know what it was like before the Obliteration, which happened just before I retired. She wasn't born until three years after it. Her project was to compare the Obliteration with the infamous 9/11 disaster almost two hundred years ago when terrorists crashed planes into the Twin Towers in New York, killing thousands of innocent civilians. It was a major event on September 11, 2001, yet you may have hardly heard about it. It changed the way of life, especially in the United States, but also to some extent worldwide. The change was from a relatively open society to a paranoid, guarded, semi-closed society focused on security. 'There hadn't been anything like that since then,' the journalist said, 'until the Obliteration.'"

Regina was now on the edge of her seat. She knew very little about the Obliteration, except that there had been a terrible explosion at the government research center where Grandpa had worked. She knew even less about the 9/11 disaster.

"I know you lived through the Obliteration, but you've never talked about it."

"You're right. I guess it's like soldiers who speak very little about their war experiences. Maybe it's survivor's guilt or just too painful. Anyway, the causes and details of 9/11 became well known. Middle Eastern terrorists crashed commercial planes filled with passengers into the Twin Towers, enormous buildings in New York, as a suicide mission. In retaliation, we invaded and bombed Afghanistan, where the terrorists trained. There was an ongoing war of sorts for about twenty years which spread to Iraq. It was a world-changing event."

"I'm surprised how little I know about all this. What will you tell the journalist about the Obliteration? It must have been awful."

He sighed heavily. "It was. I don't know if I'm going to accept her invitation. I'm not anxious to dip back into those days."

He placed his hands on his thighs.

"You've got to talk to her, Grandpa. You lived through the Obliteration."

He sighed heavily. "That's her view. She said that trying to understand past events without having lived through them was like reading gravestones in a cemetery to learn about the people buried there, and that there's renewed interest in the Obliteration, which remains a mystery today, thirty years on. Nobody knows who blew up the research center and killed so many scientists, or why they did it, or anything. Can you imagine? My name came up as a scientist working at the Vision Science Center, so she hoped that I might have some interesting thoughts about the Obliteration. She said that it was important to know what the trigger was, so it wouldn't happen again. She's an optimist."

"She's right, about it being important to know what the cause was."

"I'm reluctant. However, I admit that I'm happy that someone's interested in my view about anything. Still, when I asked her what good my perspective would be, she said that facts were 'soft,' so everyone's point of view of an event held some truth, including mine."

Regina was intrigued. Soft facts? Did the journalist mean that there was no invariant truth, just individual interpretations? When Regina stated it that way, she remembered a philosophy course where the professor had suggested that Machiavelli thought reality was only interpretation. She wondered if so-called realities were shaped by imagination rather than the facts themselves? Was reality a blur squeezed into the "wiggle" room of observations?

Ideas were floundering in Regina's mind at such a rate that she hardly heard Grandpa saying that maybe his views still had some value, that he felt the past tug at him, that perhaps he could do something to enliven his days trickling from nowhere to nowhere.

"She wanted me to go to Bethesda for the interview, to be where the Vision Science Center had been, which might awaken useful memories in me. What do you know about the research center?" he asked.

"Hardly anything," she said.

"Wait a minute. I've got some pictures to show you."

He went into his bedroom and came back with two photo albums which looked as old as the pictures they contained.

"See this huge building? That's where I worked. See this lab? That was mine. It was a busy place with students and seasoned scientists and technicians working day and night.

"I'll bet you didn't know that Ricardo Sztein, my great-great-grandfather—your ancestor too, of course—was an eye researcher at the same Vision Science Center. I worked at the same organization as the Argentinean founder of our American lineage! How's that for coincidence?"

"Wow, you're connected with Ricardo by more than genes. I didn't know he had worked at the same place you did. I know, of course, from the novel about him, *Jellyfish Have Eyes*, which I took as a biography, his far-out idea that jellyfish see evolution. That's so imaginative. I want to learn more about him."

"You're right. Ricardo was ... well, creative and innovative."

"Is that you, Grandpa," she asked, pointing to a young-looking, handsome guy.

"Sure is! Those days are gone."

He opened the other photo album filled with pictures of the entire medical center, comprising many buildings joined by roads, a few

16

memorial sculptures of scientists who had made notable contributions there, and parking lots stuffed with cars.

"It's huge, like a whole city! All that got blown up?"

"Hard to believe, isn't it? So many people killed or injured badly, and for nothing. The buildings were destroyed. It was a massive government center, a Mecca for medical and basic science research, which included the Vision Science Center."

"Do you have any pictures of how the place looked after the explosions?"

"A few."

He flipped to the back of the album and showed her two photos he'd taken before he retired to Elizabethtown. Only ruins remained, with pieces of wrecked buildings, scattered rocks, piles of bricks, deteriorating roads, and weeds everywhere. It looked like an apocalypse.

"You've got to go to Bethesda, Grandpa, and talk to that journalist. It's too important to cast off."

He scratched his thighs, fidgeted in his seat, and took a sip of his now-cold coffee.

"What would I tell the journalist?" he muttered and put the albums on the coffee table in front of the sofa.

Regina couldn't understand. Why didn't he want to be interviewed? What harm could that do? If he had been healthy and strong enough to go to her graduation, he should be well enough to go to Bethesda. Or was he right, that it would be better not to inflame old wounds? How severe were those scars? She hadn't appreciated the enormity of the traumatic experience he must have suffered. But maybe he really didn't know any more about the Obliteration than he had just told her. No. The journalist was right, she thought. Hearing about events in books, or movies, or word of mouth was completely different from being there and absorbing the event.

"How did you survive the Obliteration?"

"I was walking back from lunch just before all hell broke loose and I saw the blast at the Vision Science Center." After a short pause, he said, "It was horrible."

"My god! Were you hurt?"

"The compression waves knocked me unconscious, and a lot of

heavy stuff fell on me, but I survived, miraculously. I was in the hospital for about three months, had a couple of operations on my legs, and got sort of patched up. My shoulder still hurts, and believe it or not, I continue to feel a touch of survivor's guilt. My graduate student—she was so bright—was killed."

He sat silently staring into space, resting his tired mind.

He suddenly wandered from surviving the Obliteration to what determines destiny. He said his experience confirmed his belief that destiny depends on the way the dice roll, just plain luck, sometimes good, sometimes bad, the contingency of life. This kind of luck had nothing to do with the prepared mind, as luck has sometimes been considered. His luck had been a serendipitous "good" that day, or he would have been killed.

Regina wouldn't let him retreat into isolation. He had to accept the interview. He was still alive. She may have had her weaknesses, such as avoiding confrontations with her parents, but Grandpa was another situation. She could be more assertive when she wasn't dealing with her own issues.

"Grandpa, you shouldn't cop-out of Bethesda and the interview. You were an important scientist and are in the history books. You experienced life before the Obliteration and survived the tragedy. You owe it to the world to tell your story. The people who know the truth shouldn't hide it. Even if it's painful, those inflamed memories will simmer down to how they are now. You're going. Please."

His eyes opened wider than she had ever seen, his eyebrows shot up and wrinkled his forehead, and his jaw dropped, as if someone had squeezed his throat and cut off his oxygen supply. He appeared helpless and no longer a pillar of strength. She didn't know what was in his mind, but she couldn't miss the fact, not soft at all, that she was suddenly in control.

"What are you saying? I can't go down there by myself. What if something happens to me—if I get one of my vertigo attacks, or fall and break my leg? I'm not a spring chicken anymore. What if I have no idea what to tell that young journalist? This is very different from going with your mom and dad to see my favorite granddaughter graduate from college."

That was all she needed to hear, and she wasn't going to leave it at that. He had been her security since she was five. Now she was going to return the favor. He wasn't going to avoid life anymore. He was going to be Dr. Roger Resin, the scientist, again.

"I'm more than your favorite granddaughter," she said, in no uncertain voice. "I'm your *only* granddaughter! And you're going to the interview. Do you know how you're going to do that?

"No idea. Tell me."

"You're going with your only grandchild."

Chapter 3

G RANDPA, SPIFFY IN a gray sports jacket and blue tie, and Regina, in black pants, a pale green blouse, and black loafers, arrived a half hour before the journalist and waited for her on a bench where the Vision Science Center had been. There was nothing there but an empty field of grass with a few bare spots of dirt and a couple of semi-dead trees looking like lost, homeless victims.

Grandpa paled, as if in shock, said with a hollow voice, "There should be a plaque commemorating the many scientific and medical accomplishments achieved here, where we sit, at this very spot. Seeing this void is like meeting an apparition of a family member with a lost soul."

Regina was more objective. "If it weren't for the pictures you showed me, I wouldn't believe the biggest science research center in the world was once here. There aren't even any ruins anymore. It's just … nothing! How can history disappear so completely?"

Grandpa stared ahead and said nothing. Finally, he said. "I can't believe it either, Robin. How can such erasure of history be possible? I'm glad I never came back here after I retired. It would have been too painful, especially without you."

"Robin? I'm Regina, Grandpa, remember?"

"Sorry. Of course. I guess my mind slipped into the past. Coming back here feels like Robin should be here too. I know Robin's dead. I'm a widower, but still. I'm glad you're with me."

She understood his reluctance to return when she saw for herself the empty site of the Vision Science Center, which had been his vibrant life with his two loves: Robin and science. What would he gain by coming back to this desolate place and being interviewed by an ambitious journalist about his memories of what no longer existed and would never exist for him again? She was angry with herself for being so forceful about something she didn't know anything about. It had been hard for Grandpa at his age to come to her graduation at Princeton, which she also had pressured him to attend. But it was too late to worry about that now. They were here, in Bethesda, and she hoped it would prove to be a good thing.

It was a beautiful afternoon in the late fall, sunny, yet they shivered sitting on the dilapidated, wooden bench with flaking white chips of filthy paint sticking to their clothes.

"Are you okay, Grandpa?"

He shrugged his shoulders and scratched his thighs lightly.

"The research center—you saw the pictures—and Bethesda, were so vibrant. Now everything looks like a dull suburb. The roads seem narrow and there's so little traffic. I don't remember anything like this. The place seems dead."

"It seems kind of peaceful to me," she said.

It was close to 3:00 in the afternoon, when the journalist had said she would come. She said she would be on a bicycle wearing a tan skirt and purple blouse. It would be impossible to miss her. There was nothing to block the view, and no one else to mistake for her.

They waited.

"That must be her," said Regina as a woman approached on a bike.

"Dr. Resin?" said the journalist when she reached them. "And you're his granddaughter? Rosalie, right?"

"Regina," she said.

"And you're the mysterious journalist, correct?" Grandpa asked, knowing she was.

She nodded.

Grandpa suddenly became livelier in the presence of such an

attractive young woman with an engaging smile and dark brown eyes burning with vitality. Regina thought that the red question marks, hardly visible on the purple background of her blouse, were perfect for an interview. Hopefully she would go home with a lot of answers, or at least clarifications about the Obliteration, and possibly other things about life before the disaster as well. She would learn a lot too and was happy to be there.

"Thanks for coming, Dr. Resin. I'm very happy to meet you and your granddaughter."

"The pleasure is mine," he said. "What a desolate spot. I had no idea…"

Before he finished the sentence, the journalist asked, "Dr. Resin, how do you feel returning to the site of the Vision Science Center, now a grass field? You had mentioned that you hadn't returned here since retiring. You retired immediately after the explosion, no?"

"Yes. There was nothing left for me here, and I had reached retirement age."

"That's what I read. What memories are triggered by being here? Sorry for bombarding you with questions so soon, but I'm anxious to get your first impressions, which are often the most meaningful."

He took a deep breath, gazed up at the sky as if asking for divine assistance, and then smiled self-consciously. "My impressions? The place looks deserted compared to when I was here. Does the Metro even exist anymore?"

"It did when I was a teenager, but it was expensive to maintain and wasn't used by many people, so it's been abandoned. It's been pretty quiet here since the Obliteration."

"Doesn't anyone need to use the Metro, especially since there are so few cars on the road? Don't people go anywhere? It looks like time has regressed. This is probably what Bethesda was like fifty years before I first came here."

The journalist told him that like elsewhere, shopping was principally performed on the computer, though small stores for various personal items—gifts and novelties—remained open for limited business. There was only a single movie theater and one small bookstore.

"What about the bowling alley on … hmmm … I can't remember the name of the street. I used to go there knocking pins to smithereens."

"I don't know of any bowling alley," she said.

"Where is everyone? There's hardly anyone around."

The journalist told him that most people stayed home. "It was a combination of continued fear of terrorism after the Obliteration and fear of getting sick. There has been a string of viral diseases, some deadly, so people went out as little as possible to stay healthy. Although no connection was known, it was curious that viral illnesses became frequent after the Obliteration. The steady stream of new infectious viruses and contagious antibiotic-resistant bacteria resulted in four new hospitals that were often crowded with patients. No research was conducted there. Working at home had eroded schedules and routines. Weekends were when you decided they were.

"That's our sleepy Bethesda, Dr. Resin. It must be quite strange for you. Since I've never known anything else, it seems normal to me."

He didn't answer, but Regina said, "Bethesda looks almost like rural Elizabethtown."

The journalist changed the subject. "Shall we begin the interview? May I video record it?" she asked. "That would help me keep your words exactly as you say them and maybe use parts or all of the interview online."

Regina hesitated a moment as if she was about to object to video recording the interview, sensing that it could be a problem if he didn't have the right to approve it before making it public. But when Grandpa quickly agreed, she held back. There was no reason to question the journalist's integrity, and he seemed to like the idea. But she smelled trouble. The journalist was too polished, too obliging. It was like she had said, "first impressions are often the most meaningful."

"Why not?" he said. "I have nothing to hide. What can anyone do to me at this stage?"

The journalist clicked on her small recording machine.

"What comes first to mind when you return here?"

Regina was getting fed up with all these "firsts." What about the more thoughtful impressions, the ones most likely to be meaningful?

"Are you kidding?" he said. "What comes first to my mind when revisiting a forty-year career after a thirty-year absence?" He closed his eyes to block out the emptiness of the surroundings. "I imagine my laboratory, which was right over there." He pointed to his left. "My laboratory was staffed with a handful of postdoctoral fellows, two visiting scientists, one from Idaho and another from France at the time, a technician, and a loyal staff scientist who passed away many years ago from cancer. I see their faces in my mind. Oh, I had so many dreams then—a bundle of hopes and illusions. I don't know where to begin. I was driven with an eye toward the future in those days. Then the Obliteration came along, which reduced everything to this empty grass field with two dead—well, almost dead—trees.

"The satisfaction of teamwork comes to mind," he added. "Collaboration was important. I believe that's true for most fields—science, art, politics, crime, perhaps even the Obliteration."

"You mean that you think the Obliteration was a conspiracy, perhaps a collaboration involving a number of people?"

"I don't know. Maybe. In any case, no one thought in the same way in my laboratory. There was always someone from whom I could learn. I was a perennial student heading the laboratory. I was wearing two hats: one for the student and the other for the boss. I was learning and leading at the same time, but my goal was always to help my students. Advance their careers. My 'team'—the scientists in my laboratory—comprised multiple points of view in diverse fields of knowledge. It's like you said on the phone: the facts are soft because everyone has their own interpretation. You might say they each perceived the world through their own lens.

"The diversity guaranteed nothing, but I thought it held the ingredients for success, if put together properly. It seemed then, and still does today, that understanding the story, whatever that might be, interpreting the 'soft' facts, depends on which ones to emphasize, and what order to place them in. I remember the challenge of investigating how genes evolved and were regulated. It was an obsession. I imagined—hoped is more like it—that we took the right paths to discovery. Although there were always many possibilities and we had no template to follow, I believed, maybe now I would say I was under the illusion, that we were constructing a monument of wonder, that we explained nature and provided the foundation for the future."

Regina had heard all this in various forms many times, and it had always made her admire his idealism. She admired him now too, but it sounded different when he said it to the journalist, more like rambling about feelings than anything else. Was it wishful thinking, or perhaps his imagination pretending to be reality? Was this helpful for the journalist, who probably wasn't interested in how he conducted his research, or was it leading her astray? She was looking for causes of the Obliteration, not nostalgia from a retired scientist.

He sounded hypocritical as well as possibly replacing reality with feel-good fantasies, as a politician might talk to a journalist. Politician! The very sound of the word ... that wasn't who Grandpa was. Monument of wonder! He wasn't that pretentious. Satisfaction with teamwork! He never submerged his own significance. He respected his colleagues and wanted the best for them, but he was always Roger Resin, the ambitious head of the laboratory, with one shot to live. The confidence in himself had given her security: he was her direct support, a no-nonsense person she could trust.

He kept on speaking. "The research center was a gift to humanity and an invaluable expression of academic freedom for basic science. It never occurred to me that the research establishment wouldn't have been rebuilt after the Obliteration. I left after it was destroyed and haven't followed the politics that must have taken place, as usual. The medical research center, which included the Vision Science Center, was one of the, if not the, major medical and basic science research center in the world. Every building, including the one I worked in, was a huge beehive of activity with dozens and dozens of laboratories filled with scientists hard at work, many recognized as world authorities in their fields."

As Regina listened, she imagined Grandpa on a stage with his chest puffed up. She wasn't happy with this vision.

The journalist didn't respond. She listened. Regina wondered what she was thinking.

"It was a national treasure," he went on. "I can't believe it wasn't rebuilt even larger and better than before the Obliteration. What were they thinking, or not thinking? At the very least, they could have built a museum of medical and basic scientific history attributed to the research center, or perhaps a medical library. How sad to see a world stage as an empty grass field with two dying trees."

After a moment of silence, he asked, "What's happened to the government-supported scientific research that was here?"

The journalist did have an answer to that. "The programs that used to be funded here," she said, "are now spread among numerous smaller institutes associated with universities or medical schools. That has led to a larger and more diverse program than existed here."

Regina knew Grandpa well enough to know that he would be embarrassed that he didn't know that, probably because he had remained so isolated in Elizabethtown.

"Could anything about your research have had a connection to the sabotage of the Obliteration, even in your wildest imagination?" asked the journalist, leading the interview to its intended purpose. "For example, was there some research on germ warfare or anything else of that sort? I'm searching for anything that might be investigated further and linked to the Obliteration," said the journalist.

"No, I don't think so."

"Well, back to your research. *Did* you take the right path in your work?" the journalist asked, apparently becoming intrigued by his research.

Regina didn't trust her. She wondered what the journalist's intentions were. Was it only curiosity about his research? She thought that the journalist's effort to connect his specific research to the Obliteration was a stretch.

"There is no 'right path' in the search for knowledge," he said. "Research is a whirlpool where everything gets mixed together and it's impossible to keep a straight course. Every path leads somewhere. Right or wrong are moral issues, not a good way to think about basic research. Even so-called 'wrong paths' have value. Aren't dead ends also important to chart? The question wasn't which path to take, it was where did our chosen path take us, either by design or by accident? I chose research projects that seemed reasonable at the time, and they were always strictly about science, not terrorism or politics. Basic research is like treading water in the ocean with no shore in sight," he said. "I tried my best not to drown."

The pretty young journalist was writing down what he said as well as recording it, clearly wanting to remember everything for her article.

"I'm looking for something that I hope has at least some chance to connect with the Obliteration," said the journalist for the umpteenth time. "Do you know of any research that went on at that time that a terrorist might target?"

Regina also wondered why Grandpa couldn't get that message. The journalist was interested in the Obliteration, not his research and career.

"No. I kept my nose to the grindstone. Do you think that Thought-Particles with evil messages of revenge from a paranoid scientist who believed he was discriminated against might have planted the seed to some crazy individual or terrorists?"

The journalist ignored those comments and continued her questioning. "Dr. Resin, I understand the complexity and interrelationships of everything, making all choices, which you call paths, have some value. But really, sir, aren't some ideas of what to follow more correct, or at least more productive, than others? Are there any thoughts that might come to you about the Obliteration? That didn't seem important to you then? Sorry to keep repeating myself, but I'm looking for some path that might guide me to the heart of the Obliteration. Who is to blame? Why? What was the cause? It's like your research. No one knows the answer; it's been thirty years, yet no one has a clue of what happened to cause the Obliteration. Can you imagine how unacceptable and dangerous that would have been with respect to 9/11 way back then? One can't just wave the white flag, allowing people who are responsible to repeat such acts, or even do worse ones. We need to find something that takes us to answers about the Obliteration."

Grandpa nodded as if he agreed with the journalist, but he didn't respond.

A wave of uncertainty flowed over Regina. She would have liked to help him answer some of the questions that the journalist asked, but she knew almost nothing about the Obliteration. Also, while she knew a little about Grandpa's Thought-Particles, she didn't think they were relevant. Why wouldn't he leave them alone now? He seemed to cling to his disappointment that Thought-Particles were never accepted by his colleagues. She hadn't realized how much anger he still had about that. But conflating that personal problem with the Obliteration? How could that help the journalist? Had she made a mistake in urging him to agree to the interview?

"Look," he said, "why don't you pick something that was troublesome at the time—political issues, countries antagonistic to ours, animal rights or pro-choice groups—and go from there. I know, there are many possibilities, and it was long ago. Still, when revisiting imaginary rainbows, there might be a pot of gold at the end of one. Every time I investigated one idea, I found that it raised other questions that required answers, and these questions delved into different areas of science, some I understood, and others I didn't have a clue how to follow up. Many times, I took detours I never realized I was taking. It was all about … about what? *Sleepwalking*. Yes, that's it. I was sleep-walking in a foreign country without a map. I didn't know quite where I wanted to go or why. Was there even an explanation? Did infectious Thought-Particles really exist? That question has haunted me since I dreamed them up. Did they exist? Surely someone will identify them in the future."

Regina's face reddened as her anger mounted. Didn't he have more self-control to limit this disjointed barrage to the journalist? Thought-Particles and the Obliteration were separate issues! She was embar-rassed and mad and sad and confused and worried about his lack of discipline.

He stopped rambling when he noticed her frustrated glance and asked in a quiet voice, "Should we go someplace to get a cup of coffee?"

"In a moment," said the journalist, who had displayed considerable patience. "I still hope you will touch on the Obliteration eventually. I understand how disorienting it must be for you to return here after such a long hiatus. Let time run backward. Think again whether you might have heard or considered anything concerning the Obliteration, no matter how irrelevant it may have seemed then or now. Perhaps a phrase or a casual thought may turn out to be important." The journalist gazed at the barren terrain and shook her head. "I've heard conflicting and conspiracy stories, but not by anyone who actually lived through it."

"I don't think I know much more about the Obliteration than you do," Grandpa said.

"I've read everything I could find on the Obliteration," she said. "Possibilities and rumors abound, but nothing was consistent or convincing. That's why I want to hear what you went through. Sometimes grassroots suggest the best answers."

After a short silence, he said, "You know, maybe I can think of some unlikely things that may be interesting, but my mind is a blur now. Let me think about it and see what I can come up with tomorrow."

The journalist smiled enthusiastically. "Great. Let's meet tomorrow at your hotel at nine for breakfast and we can talk about it? In the meantime, I'd like to invite you to an early dinner at my favorite restaurant, SynFood."

"Does the name mean the food is sinful, like rich chocolate desserts?" Regina asked, hoping that would be the case.

"No, no. Quite the opposite. It's not s-i-n; it's s-y-n, for synthetic food. It's very healthy, and not bad either. I think you'll like it."

Regina had heard about synthetic food—like what space travelers ate.

"Don't worry. I bet it's tasty," Grandpa said.

The restaurant was almost empty, which the journalist said was because most of their business was delivery service, not because the food was not good. Synthesized food was a growing business. Vegetables, meat products low in fat and without cholesterol, and an assortment of sugar-free desserts were available as pills and sponge-like substances with different flavors. Some pharmacies even delivered "prescription meals." Regina had read that fifteen to twenty per cent of the people eat synthetic food, and a few more eat a mixture of synthetic and "real" food.

Grandpa looked disoriented by the strange new world. Regina too said little and had no idea what to order from the menu. The journalist suggested that they order the chef's combination special for three.

"Perfect," said Regina, willing to take a chance.

She had no better knowledge of what she had eaten after the meal than she had while eating it, and had no interest in knowing the names of each course, which she considered medical regimes.

Grandpa, more to the point than he had been during the interview, said, "It was no meat and potatoes!"

Chapter 4

Later, at the hotel, Regina discussed the afternoon with Grandpa. The journalist was pleasant enough, they agreed, but they thought she was looking for needles in a haystack. Regina told Grandpa that he should keep his remarks connected with the Obliteration and cool it on Thought-Particles. They agreed that seeing the grass lawn with its two dying trees was more depressive than impressive, yet it was worth the trip. Grandpa also thought the government diversifying the research that used to be based at the medical center was a good idea, and a clever way to increase the funding and at the same time protect it from sabotage. Diversity was safer than centralization.

Grandpa was astounded by the major changes in Bethesda: a deterioration from his point of view. "Seeing it is the only way I would have believed it. It seems that there is little pleasure in life anymore. No socialization, no exploring new places, and food just a series of medicines. And still, we all die as before, although it's true the average lifespan has been increased, but not by enough as far as I'm concerned. What else do you think the journalist will tell us about this world? Do you think life will return to what I call normal?"

"I doubt it, Grandpa, but I'm not a soothsayer. What about the vague thoughts you mentioned you might have that might relate to the Obliteration? Were you wishing you had something that might be relevant, or were you trying to escape her constant questions, or a little of each?"

"I don't know. It was a blur. Maybe a little of both." He paused and rubbed his chin as a substitute for saying something relevant.

"Tell me. I'm not the journalist. It doesn't matter what you say to me."

"Okay, I'll try. But don't laugh. Do you dream a lot?"

"Dream? Of course. Doesn't everyone?"

"I suppose. But maybe not like I do."

"What's that supposed to mean?"

"I'm embarrassed to tell you, but it's on my mind, as if that might be telling me something. I don't know why …"

"Just tell me, okay?"

"All right. Relax. I saw this movie a couple of nights ago called *Real Dreams*. The movie implied that the dreams were based on some reality, a reality that could prophesize the future. That's not a new thought, but it's still an interesting one. What do you think?"

"How would I know? I've never even heard of the movie."

"Often in the past, I didn't know if my dreams were camouflaged reality or just fantasy. Crazy, huh? Anyway, in *Real Dreams* the protagonist had repetitive dreams about murdering his neighbor—shot him at night when he saw him out for a walk—so he could seduce his wife. With every repetition some new fact or twist was revealed. It was a labyrinth of complexity. But here's the important part. The protagonist murdered the guy, just as the dream said he did. The simplest interpretation is that the dream was his wish and it pushed him to make it come true. Isn't that sort of fantasy, wishful thinking and reality, all combined? The murdered guy was an outstanding person, liked by everyone—a judge, no less. The protagonist—the murderer—was lonely. His wife died of cancer in her forties, and he had a crush on his neighbor's wife. Like I said: he was lonely."

"Some crush! Did he get caught? Did he seduce his neighbor's wife? Sounds like a juicy film."

"Yes, entertaining. He did get caught, like a fly in a spider's web that the police set for him. It was a movie, right? It needed a clever ending. The woman married one of the cops that caught the murderer. How's that for irony?"

"Clever, as you said."

Regina was perplexed. Talking about a movie she hadn't seen couldn't possibly be what he thought might help the journalist on her quest to understand the Obliteration.

"What does this movie have to do with the Obliteration?" she asked.

"Well, I dream a lot. I mean *a lot*, almost every night. I always did, way before Grandma Robin died. My dreams were and still are ridiculously detailed. When they wake me up, I'm often convinced the dream was a real happening, that I was part of the action in some way, which of course I wasn't. Yet dreams have a life of their own, like any story. It's larger than the person dreaming or of the artist's creation or of the scientist's discovery. The messenger is not the substance. What I dream isn't me, whether it's fantasy or reality. I've even gotten out of bed and believed that I'm still in the dream, sort of like being aware that I'm sleepwalking. Sometimes I woke Robin and asked her about something connected with the dream, like does she know where the knife in my dream is, which wouldn't make any sense to her. She would reassure me that I just had a dream; it wasn't real. 'It was a *dream*,' she would insist, without any doubts whatsoever. I didn't always believe her since the dream seemed so real, so specific, so detailed, so graphic ... so *real*. I imagine that I felt like someone having a halluci-nation who is convinced that the image *is* real—scary real. I hallucinate too sometimes. I see spiders in my mind scampering all over the place. They're mostly black, but sometimes red. It's frightening, even though I know that they aren't real, or at least, they better not be real! My dreams often feel real or about reality of some kind, more real than my hallucinations. Sometimes the dreams are frightening, but sometimes they are pleasant, even comforting, and I want them to continue. They are a way to live vicariously, an alternative event in my life, an oppor-tunity to inhabit my imagination."

He was agitated, waving his arms around.

Regina's eyes narrowed as if she was confused or did not know what to say. She decided to take this one step further.

"Grandpa, tell me exactly about the dream or dreams you're

recalling. You said they were vivid, as if they were reality. Give me the details."

Regina wanted the facts. She was already a scientist at heart.

"That's the problem. The dreams I'm thinking of telling the journalist about happened very long ago, soon after the Obliteration."

Regina looked puzzled. "You want to tell her about your dreams from thirty years ago and you have a hard time remembering exactly what they were about?"

"Well, I'm not sure. It's sort of muddled in my mind. Well, here goes. I had a strange, complex, repetitive dream that had several parts, or maybe they were separate dreams. One part was about Middle Eastern terrorists delivering desks in a truck and planting explosives in the Vision Science Center. When they left, they triggered the explosions remotely through some electronic device, and an alarm alerted the police, who located them with GPS. They followed the trucks and killed the drivers with machine guns. It was a bloody massacre."

"Wow! I like it!" Regina said, making no secret of her bent for violence, which surprised Grandpa.

"Hold on, Regina. Another part of the dream had a cult of a dozen men with igloo tattoos on their necks. They entered the campus, planted the explosives, and got away. The dream didn't say how the gunpowder was set off."

"Igloo tattoos? These dreams would make great movies or novels. Can I record all this? Excuse me. I mean video record."

He ignored her and went on. "Why igloos? Maybe because the Arctic is so remote and mysterious, like the Obliteration, or maybe because I especially liked Inuit art at that time. Maybe the tattoos weren't of igloos but some other kind of sign. When I awoke, I tried to remember whether the truck drivers also had these tattoos, or any tattoos at all, that might link the two different dreams. A third part of the dream was a pipe leaking gas, which caused an explosion. That's all, just an image of a pipe and a hissing sound of the escaping gas. Sometimes all three parts happened in one dream, or sometimes only one or two of the parts occurred."

"What's the big deal?" she said. "Lots of people have dreams that psychologists and scientists and just about everyone try to interpret.

Wait, I'm confused. Do you want to tell the journalist about these dreams, or that you heard about these events from some source, or what?"

Grandpa hesitated. "Something like that. She seems desperate to have some clue to follow up. I have no idea whether these dreams mean anything at all. They probably don't. But maybe they do. Maybe I heard rumors somewhere or saw them in a documentary. It may all be nonsense—probably is—but it may also have some truth. The journalist is smart. I think she might too smart for her own good, or that she thinks she's smart and can dig deeper than anyone else. Well, whatever. I don't know. She would take what she wants from my dreams and leave the rest. Maybe she'll look for articles or some source from news or rumors of that time which she can try to link with my dreams about the Obliteration. Who knows? At least it's something. After all, dreams must come from some real source. Wouldn't it be possible that my dreams, at least in part, relate to the Obliteration? That would be something, don't you think?"

"You've got to be kidding, Grandpa? Are you losing your grip on reality?"

He scratched his thighs lightly and said, "Do you really think it's that preposterous, Regina? Do you think it's more preposterous than the Obliteration itself? People have spent thirty years getting nowhere in the search for its cause. What harm can an unlikely long-shot do?"

"No, no, no! You can't get mixed up in all this craziness with old dreams you barely remember! No! Please no! Tell her you can't help her, that you're tired and are going home. We'll go back home tomorrow."

After Regina said this her mind started churning—not on whether these fanciful dreams had some truth, or whether he should relate them to the journalist, but whether she wanted to write a story about them. If nothing else, they might make interesting fiction. She would ask Grandpa if he minded. His dreams were certainly original!

He agreed to both, going home and her writing a story about his dreams. The journalist said she understood and thanked him, but also said, "If you think of anything, Dr. Resin, anything at all, please get in touch with me. We can also videoconference if that would be helpful."

They were back in Elizabethtown the next day.

Chapter 5

REGINA REFLECTED THAT evening about Grandpa's dreams and the Obliteration. Both remained clouded in mystery. It didn't make sense in a technology-oriented universe where everything—news, gossip—was spread electronically worldwide. Lack of information was hardly an issue. Too much information and too many opinions were greater problems. The truth about the Obliteration was probably buried in the morass of information but too difficult to tease out because of all the extraneous information and contradictions and fake news, especially with time distorting the memories. Could there be a world without a common reality, a world that was viewed as possibilities and illusions that substituted for universal truth? That would make reality embedded in fiction, as in novels and stories. Fiction needs some connection or credibility to common experiences—an accepted reality—to be believable.

Imagination/Fiction/Reality. These reverberated in Regina's head.

She decided to write a story—fiction—about an explosion. Grandpa had agreed that it would be okay to use his dreams for a story, so why not? That would be fun and who knows, wouldn't it be amazing if Grandpa's wild dreams turned out to help understand the Obliteration? As they say, "truth is stranger than fiction." Grandpa did say there were rumors about the Obliteration. What were those? He hadn't mentioned them. Maybe rumors he had heard were the source of his dreams. A story of hers might make him remember the rumors.

She didn't want to belittle the Obliteration in a story, which would be in poor taste, if not disrespectful. However, an inconclusive story— taking the trouble to write Grandpa's dreams— might make her think about the Obliteration differently, which was what Grandpa had thought when he'd considered telling the journalist the dreams. Not everything was a clear truth or fiction. There was always a blurring, or cracks in the story, where imagination ruled. An imaginative story could be suggestive—unproven but novel, like Grandpa's Thought-Particles. Stories often became real in her mind, but that didn't mean they were real. Fiction and reality played on each other.

Yes, she would write a story, a fantasy she would entitle *Destruction*, that fictionalized Grandpa's dreams. Writers often revisit ideas and plots of what others had written. Similarly, scientists repeat others' experiments to verify the conclusions and go a step further, and student painters copy the work of masters. Shakespeare wrote plays—fiction— about history, and he did all right! She could *believe* her story was true if she wanted to, and belief was essential for credibility.

"I'll do it," she muttered, getting excited to start. She would write a short story in her room, now, surrounded by all her favorite things—the framed title page of a story she'd written in third grade, her collection of novels, the microscope she received as a teenager. She turned on her computer and started a story about a hospital destroyed by an explosion told from the point of view of a survivor relating the tragedy to a clueless young journalist who wasn't even born until a few years after the event. She wanted her imagination to creep into Grandpa's mind. Also, she thought that writing a story directly from what Grandpa told her might create enough distance for both her and him to see it more clearly; the freedom of fiction could allow truth to be seen from different perspectives.

She started to write.

Destruction: Truth or Fantasy?

"Do you have any idea what actually happened?" the journalist asked the survivor, Trixie, many years after the fact. "You were there ... right here ... at this very spot, where the hospital was. The journalist looked baffled as he gazed at the now barren terrain. "I've heard conflicting stories, but not by anyone who actually lived through it."

No one knew exactly what happened or the cause of the explosion. It was like the event had disappeared into a sinkhole. Trixie couldn't add much to what was commonly known, which wasn't much, about the Destruction, as it was called. She was just grateful not to have been killed. Many of her colleagues and patients were killed. She would try her best to blend her memories with what she heard, although they were just rumors. Oh, blessed imagination! What would she do without it? Also, she figured, where there's smoke, there's fire, so perhaps the rumors had some truth.

"Here's one possibility I've heard," she told the journalist.

A documentary—Big Blast—was popular at the time but was soon removed from circulation because it lacked proof and was criticized as misleading. It was widely regarded as propaganda, a blurring of truth and fiction. Its conclusions were elusive—maybe this, maybe that—as if there was no satisfactory explanation. Even when "certainty" was declared with passion, another side to the story popped up, another way of looking at the evidence, another so-called "truth," so she figured there was little risk in telling the journalist a tale that may or may not have some truth in it. In any case, the journalist had implied that the multiple perspectives were as numerous as the people who had them, and that the same facts could lead to different conclusions. Maybe the Destruction was fiction, a nightmare. Maybe what appeared to happen was a dream.

Unlikely. Or maybe not. The movie looked real.

"Big Blast *opened with a delivery truck going to security at the rear of the hospital to deliver several desks. A security guard had to inspect the truck to clear the delivery. There was a passenger with the driver.*

"Please open your hood and the back door of the truck," the inspector commanded.

"No problem," answered the driver, politely. Almost too politely. Obsequiously.

The guard gave the impression of being a fascist, although that was a subjective opinion based on his stiff and authoritative manner. Perhaps that's how it works, Trixie thought: everything is presented as routine, as the vise closes slowly, until ... until it's too late. The driver snapped both the hood and the back door open with the touch of the switch.

"What's in the back?" asked the guard.

"Desks," answered the driver. The shortest direct answer was the least incriminating.

"Mind if I take the cover off one or two of these ... desks ... and check?" The guard was polite and respectful if you didn't cross him. Nonetheless, he carried a revolver on his belt, and there was always a backup guard, also armed, just in case.

"Suit yourself, officer."

The guard removed the canvas covers from two desks, tapped the desktops with a small hammer to see if they were hollow, opened a drawer at random, and inspected the interior of the truck with a flashlight. He swabbed a few areas to look for traces of gunpowder with their sensitive detectors.

"Go on, buddy," said the guard. "Good luck unloading all that stuff! Glad that's not my job!" The documentary had small touches like that to make it relatable for the common man.

The truck advanced to the loading dock and the two men got out carrying a few small sacks retrieved from under the passenger seat, which the guard hadn't noticed. Too bad. The sacks were filled with a powerful explosive that tested negative for conventional gunpowder. They were bombs, at least presumably, that could be detonated by remote control from a distance up to five miles. The men planted the sacks in various places in the hospital. They put the desks on the dock and drove away. The documentary scanned the halls of the hospitals showing immigrants dressed in foreign-looking clothes. They spoke a potpourri of languages, implying a smorgasbord of nationalities.

The truck drove north, staying well within the speed limit. Everything seemed like a regular day's business. But it wasn't. When the truck was about four miles away, the driver, a foreigner in his mid-thirties, pressed a remote-control apparatus and ... BANG! The hospital was destroyed.

Within minutes of the explosions, police officers, with sirens screaming, caught up to the truck and emptied their machine guns on the driver and passenger, assuming they were the villains. Rat-a-tat-tat! Rat-a-tat-tat! End of driver and passenger, the presumed terrorists killed. Justice was served. USA. USA. The case was closed.

Yes, indeed. Big Blast showed that the world was a dangerous place, no slice of American apple pie. You couldn't be too careful!

"Fascinating," said the journalist. "I'll write that up."

"Not so quick," said Trixie. "A news report challenged the documentary and said the desk delivery story wasn't reliable. It was never proved that the sacks contained explosives, and the delivery men were never observed directly hiding the sacks in several places. Moreover, the police attack on the truck was apparently taken from another incident. In short, there wasn't a scrap of direct evidence incriminating the truck drivers. The movie could have been fiction made for entertainment and profit.

A second scenario of the Destruction was, ironically, taken from the same documentary but told a completely different story.

At the lower right-hand corner of the movie screen a dozen men could be seen passing security to the hospital. The men looked respectable, dressed in slacks, shirts with open collars and sports *jackets. Very spiffy. They were loosely organized in three pairs of two, one threesome, and two trailing, one behind the other. They didn't look like either employees or patients. Each was carrying a satchel larger than a briefcase but smaller than a suitcase. The contents of the satchels weren't disclosed since they passed the electronic check. There were small tattoos on the right earlobes of seven of the men (the right ears of the other five were not visible in the movie) that resembled igloos, possibly with evil spirits escaping from blocks of ice. That was, of course, guesswork. But there it was: another mystery. Who were these guys?*

A member of the tattooed group waved to one of the security guards, who returned the greeting. What did that mean? A collaboration, or just acquaintances, or neither? This friendly exchange may have been a ruse to show how harmless the group was, which implied the attack may have been an inside job. Were these guys the villains, or were the truck delivery men guilty, or neither?

Trixie got excited when she told this account, and for whatever reason, she told the journalist, "I bet it was the pedestrians, not the truck guys, poor dead souls. The pedestrians didn't have ID badges hanging from their necks, and what was in the satchels? Very suspicious. They even marched (a little militaristic language, she knew, but …) into the hospital. There were more pedestrians than cars, so it was probably easier to pass security on foot. They were inspected at the checkpoint, but what happened there wasn't shown. There were no clues in the demolished building.

Trixie's preference—guess—was that the dozen men with tattoos on their right earlobes went past security with explosives that couldn't be detected electronically in their briefcases, walked into the hospital, hid the explosives in various spots, walked out, and WHAMO!

The documentary ended with a river of American flags flowing across the screen, left to right with subliminal images of George Washington, Abraham Lincoln, Theodore Roosevelt, Woodrow Wilson, Franklin D. Roosevelt, George W. Bush, Barack Obama, and Donald Trump, all past presidents during wars and terrorism of one sort or another.

"Whew! What a mess of riddles. Quite a story. It would make a good novel or soap opera," said the journalist. "Do you know where I might ... "

"Oh, wait," Trixie said, suddenly remembering another theory. "Two survivors checked with the utilities department in Bethesda. The officials told them that the explosion wasn't sabotage, in their opinion, but due to a gas leak. Many laboratories in the hospital had access to natural gas. It was not possible to check the gas lines for leaks after the fact since all the pipes were destroyed.

"So," the journalist said. "Total confusion. Perhaps sabotage; maybe not. Foreign terrorists or some crazy cult, possibly in cahoots with the security guards, or an accident due to leaking gas—no one guilty. Maybe the police were involved and killed the truck driver and his passenger to prevent them from squealing. Or maybe not."

"Yup, that's about it," said Trixie.

The journalist closed his notebook, put his pen back in his pocket, raised his eyebrows and said, politely of course, "Fuck it."

"It beats the movies, wouldn't you say?" said Trixie, smiling. "If you search for the most imaginative fiction, just look at the confusion of truth! It kind of gave me chills when I saw that movie. I don't know what's true, but the movie producers sure know their business."

"I haven't heard any of these strange ideas about the Destruction. Are you making up these stories?" asked the journalist.

"No, no. Heavens no," Trixie replied.

Regina wrote the story in less than an hour. Her fingers had rushed across the keyboard like Olympic sprinters, and then she capped the end with a final period. She realized that a concluding sentence was not the best ending for her fantasy, which didn't conclude. Franz Kafka's dystopian novel *The Castle* ended in the middle of a sentence, for it too had no conclusion. Stories often ended ambiguously, the richest source of the many perspectives that always exist. If she ever published this story, she would end it mid-sentence.

She was excited by her story. She did love to write, and this connection with Grandpa was especially meaningful. Wanting his opinion, she sent it to him electronically with a note in capital letters he couldn't miss: *DO YOU LIKE IT?*

When Regina was lying in the dark half asleep, she drifted back to her story. It was a mixture of fiction and fantasy, with her mind on a journey of imagination. She wondered if imagination and reality could work together, and if so, in what way? Diverse facts never amounted to a single story that excluded other possible interpretations. Coherence, but not necessarily the only perspective, depended on linking facts by trial and error. The same story could be weaved into many possible stories with different endings by dreaming up different ways to link the facts or adding a new fact or two along the way, as was the case in science where new observations continually modified the existing truth or perspective. Absolute truth, if it existed at all, was a fragile house of cards, as described in *Destruction*.

She wondered once again whether an understanding of the Obliteration was buried under information overload due to all the technical innovations. Was she living in a world of reality, or was she in the middle of a nightmare? If the latter, when would she wake up? *Would* she wake up?

With these disturbing thoughts she drifted off to sleep and dreamed of a younger, angry Grandpa. He disappeared from her dream and was replaced by two truck drivers with tattoos on their necks, and in a different scene, a dozen foreign-looking pedestrians, all men, walking towards an immense building with VSC written on it. The pedestrians had tattoos on their earlobes that looked like those on the men in the truck. It was unclear what the tattoos were about, but she speculated that they looked like igloos. The scene suddenly changed to a large building exploding and bodies flying in all directions. It was horrifying. Grandpa was lying on the ground in a pool of blood, maybe dead, maybe still alive, barely. The pale head of a stranger with protruding eyes—no body was visible—appeared, saying, "Truth fluctuates as the grapevine grows wild in different directions."

Grandpa re-entered the dream looking older, maybe a hundred, his face wrinkled, his gaze directed at the ground. He said that documentaries should be banned if they gave equal weight to all competing possibilities, such as proclaiming that God and genetics are equal theories for evolution, as some people preach. Could we "genius" humans have really evolved from dumb monkeys or any other animal, such skeptics asked?

Suddenly she, Regina, appeared in the dream in the tan skirt and purple blouse with question marks that the pretty young journalist wore. Thought-Particles as tiny hexagons rained from above. There was no division between earth and sky: everything was colored bland blue. She was smiling. Grandpa was dancing. Mom and Dad, appearing indifferent, floated out of sight. She could discern the outline of another universe, something different, in the distance, with sharp edges that overlapped the universe she was in. What universe was in the distance, and which one was she in?

"Regina, wake up! It's after noon. You've been asleep so long I got scared. You said you would do some errands and shopping for me this morning and it's already the afternoon."

Regina stretched and yawned. "I'm fine, Mom. Just dreaming."

Her first thought was her story, not the errands. Maybe she would expand it to a novella or a novel someday.

Chapter 6

Regina bounded into Grandpa's house, anxious to know if he'd had a chance to read her story.

"I did as soon as you sent it to me. It's a good fictional representation of my dreams. You got the characters and flavor right. Good work, Queen Regina! But reading it made me feel strange, like being on the outskirts of my own reality. I liked the ambiguous ending, making the cause of the Destruction as impossible to determine as it has been for the Obliteration in real life."

She beamed. To hear such praise from Grandpa meant a great deal to her.

"Thanks, Grandpa. There's nothing I prefer more than a respected reader—especially you—liking what I wrote. I guess we all like recognition. For writers it's especially important because their stories are subjective, not objective like science. It's all about liking or not liking."

Grandpa rubbed his jaw. "It's not entirely objective for the scientist either," he said. "There's plenty of room for subjectivity and self-promotion in science too."

It was clear to Regina, as it was when Grandpa spoke to the journalist, that he was still frustrated that his non-existent Imagination gene needed to be retracted when he was starting out in research, and, most of all, that his precious Thought-Particles theory was drifting incognito somewhere in the cosmos.

Grandpa asked Regina what she planned to do with her story.

Yes, she wondered. Did she plan to submit it for publication in a journal? If so, did she want to submit it as such or expand it into a novella or novel first? The story was drawn from his dreams. How should she acknowledge him? Just say that she had just written his story? Wasn't that plagiarism? Should she say anything about the Obliteration? Probably not.

"Of course, I will acknowledge you if it's published someday," she said. "However, if I said that the story was based on your dream about the Obliteration, it would be doing what I told you not to bring up to the journalist. Publishing would make it even more confusing than having told her about it, as you wanted to do, since there would be no documented statement that could be traced back to you in that case. Maybe I was too quick to discourage you from telling your dreams to the journalist, but I still think it was the right decision."

He leaned over, cradled his head with his hands, and mumbled to himself loud enough for her to hear, "Why am I always so impulsive before I think things through? I never seem to learn."

He sighed, and then added, "I shouldn't have done it, or at least I should have waited, thought it through, got your opinion."

Regina bolted straight up in her chair. "What are you saying, Grandpa? Shouldn't have done what? Waited for what? Got my opinion on what?"

He looked directly into her eyes with a sense of alarm.

"What's the problem, Grandpa?"

"Please don't be mad, but I sent your story to the journalist yesterday since I thought it represented precisely what my dreams were about. I wanted to know whether it would be of any interest to her. I know you didn't want to do that when we were in Bethesda, but what harm could it do? How would I, or anyone at this point, know if those dreams had cryptic information that might help reveal a clue to the Obliteration?

"My dreams were real, but I don't know where they came from. Maybe I had some relevant information that I didn't know I had. What was their source? It's hard to believe that I made them up from a vacuum. I wanted to know whether she thought that the dreams had enough merit for her to pursue further to understand the Obliteration.

I should have talked to you about it first. I was impulsive, as always. Often, I feel if I don't react to impulse, I won't act at all. Sorry."

Regina scrunched her face as if angry, but at the same time softened her gaze as if she understood. He was being vintage Grandpa; what did she expect? People don't change very often, if ever. He always was impulsive and frustrated; her parents didn't seem to care about her very much. No one becomes someone else.

"Well, what's done is done, Grandpa. Let's see what the journalist says. My bet is she will thank you and discard it. I wouldn't know where to start if I received such a story to investigate further to solve a crime or a mysterious event like the Obliteration."

"Hope you're right, Regina. As soon as I clicked the *send* key on my computer, I got worried. I feel a little better now that I've told you that I sent it."

Regina listened without expression, believing, or at least hoping, that Grandpa hadn't opened a can of worms that would cause trouble. But what could that be? Probably nothing. Why would, or how could, the journalist follow up a story based on somebody's dream of thirty years ago? It didn't make sense. She also was wondering if she should let the journalist know that she wrote the story and was thinking of keeping it unpublished and confidential. Then Grandpa hit her with another bombshell.

Chapter 7

"THERE'S MORE, REGINA. I don't know what got into me but ... your story isn't all I sent the journalist."

"More, Grandpa? Really? Why? What did you tell her? Was it by phone or videoconferencing?"

"Videoconferencing. I know, videoconferencing has been going on forever. But do you have any idea how sophisticated it has become? It used to be that people could talk and see each other on the screen. But now the digital participants can step out of the screen, it's possible to have digital persons, illusions, like hallucinations, holograms, but with a will of their own—they can visit anyone's home or do 'face-to-face' business transactions. It's the same as dealing with people directly, except that the digital person out of the screen is a 'fake' reality, alive in some sense, and yet not."

Regina was taken aback. Where did Grandpa's surprises end?

"Wasn't there a fantasy movie like that in the twentieth century?" she said. "I love old movies and it's coming back to me. Woody Allen, what a character he was, made a movie called *The Purple Rose of Cairo* in which the main guy, an archaeologist I think, stepped out of the screen to join a depressed waitress. That was pure imagination then. Now you're saying that can really happen. I didn't know that."

"Yeah, the journalist did just that. Didn't I tell you that imagination can come true on occasion? I experienced this, more than once.

It's my hope for Thought-Particles, and it's a good reason not to be too quick to dispense with an idea."

"Still thinking of Thought-Particles, Grandpa?"

"I suppose, a little. Accept it, Regina, Woody Allen's movie fantasy is now a reality. The journalist told me it was even possible for the same digital person to step out in more than one place, making it possible to be at several places at the same time. Isn't that wild?"

As Regina was taking all this in, she started thinking about the ramifications of videoconferencing with digital individuals stepping in and out of the screen and visiting multiple people, sort of like being cloned. Imagine the possibilities and/or complications for making business deals, or for politics, or even for writing. Direct contradictions could be enacted simultaneously, and so-called truth would become as useless as so-called fake news. Life would become a fairy tale, a work of fiction, and hopelessly ambiguous, so that no interpretation of anything was either true or false, depending on who is telling you what and from where. Fact and illusion would be indistinguishable. Nobody would know for certain if the "person" talking to them was real or digital—the persons themselves might not even know if they were real or digital.

Grandpa was in a playground of imagination and seemed to be loving every minute of it.

"Stop!" Unlike Grandpa, Regina was in a flurry of confusion and increasingly worried about his state of mind, and more importantly, about what he had told the journalist. "Forget the philosophy for a minute, Grandpa, and tell me what you said to the journalist, or to her digital image. I assume she stepped out of the videoconference?"

"She did. At first I saw her on the computer screen, and then suddenly she was sitting on the chair you're in now. However, her image was still on the screen as well. She was like a computer alias, a clone, as I said, present on the screen and out of it too."

"Do you think the image of her on the chair was a projected hologram?"

"Maybe. But it's really the same thing, wouldn't you say? We talked to each other as if she were here in the flesh. That's the fact."

Fact? thought Regina. Perhaps a "soft" fact. Was the journalist's digital image really her? How many aliases did she have out there?

Regina saw Grandpa in a different light than in the past. Was he becoming senile, perhaps in the beginning stages of Alzheimer's or another degenerative illness? She didn't know what to expect from him anymore. Exactly who was Grandpa now?

"Grandpa, tell me what you told the journalist."

"I told her about my parents."

Chapter 8

"**Y**OUR PARENTS? WHY did you bring them up? They don't seem relevant. I don't even see how she could fit them into an article about the Obliteration."

Stop it, Regina said to herself, and let Grandpa say what happened.

He fidgeted and drank some coffee. He was always drinking coffee, he lived on coffee and evaded life on coffee—maybe he would die drinking coffee, the miracle drug. Regina sensed that he didn't want to tell her what he said to the journalist. But that wasn't her decision. No, she thought. He never kept secrets from her, and she felt that he knew he needed her. He wouldn't continue if he didn't want to.

"Okay, Regina. Here we go again. I bet you'll write a story about all this some time."

"Did you ever doubt it?" She smiled.

Grandpa said that the journalist wondered whether his reactions or memories about the Obliteration might have been influenced by his upbringing—his family and how he dealt with adversity.

"Well, what did you tell her? I thought you were raised by your mother, since your father skipped town when you were a baby."

Regina was getting impatient and wanted him to get to the point. Did his confusion about dreams and what he remembered or told the journalist make sense? His whole interview adventure started to sound like facts mixed with imagination, plus some confusion with age. Maybe it would all come together eventually.

"My father deserted us, yes," Grandpa said. "But there's a lot more I never told you."

He told her that his father reappeared, terminally sick with Lou Gehrig's Disease—amyotrophic lateral sclerosis, as it was called—which was whittling his life away, layer by layer.

"It was ironic and bad timing, Regina. I got to know my father right after I received my Ph.D. and was starting my life and he was pitifully sick, ending his. I felt I couldn't leave my mother to deal with that horrible situation by herself, so I stayed a while."

"What did you do?" Regina asked, wondering if she would make such a sacrifice of time for her mother or father. Probably not. She didn't cancel her appointments to take care of Mom when she had the flu and was home alone a few years ago.

"I wasn't sure what to do, but I wanted to be useful in whatever way I could. I passed up several tempting offers for jobs at universities to stay where I was needed. I watched him get worse, bit by bit, but I couldn't do anything about it."

He gave Regina a strange look, almost self-conscious. "Do you understand?"

Regina touched his arm sympathetically, lightly, with tenderness, her brown eyes softening. "I'm so sorry," she said. "You must have been crushed after your father died."

"He died slowly. It would have been better for both of us if it had been quicker."

"Sounds grim. How did your mom take it?"

"Hard to say. She was an actor and used to playing all kinds of roles, including sad and tragic ones involving death, but I'm sure it wasn't easy for her."

Grandpa clenched his jaw, and the creases on his forehead deepened as he related the torment. "I would have preferred to have no image of my father rather than that of a suffering, twisted, miserable waste of a man who didn't care enough about me even to send a birthday card."

Regina was silent in sympathy for a moment, remembering that her parents once forgot her birthday. She admitted to herself that she had wished they—especially her father—were dead at times.

"When he was deteriorating in a wheelchair, we were able to talk about ourselves, and for the first time I thought of him as Dad. ALS was a dark gift to me in that way."

A dad is different from a father, thought Regina. I've had a dad all my life, but never felt he was a supportive father.

Grandpa paused. "But when my father became Dad, with a capital D, he still lashed out at me for not accepting reality and kept hammering that I, a scientist, lived in a dream world, not in reality. He meant *his* reality, that is, not mine. He was a stockbroker and kept repeating like a parrot that I had to make money, that life wasn't a dream, it was real, not like science, which seemed to be mostly playing with technical instruments and fanciful ideas. He said I was a tinkerer, not a provider. Can you believe it, Regina? He gave me the idea that I didn't know the difference between dreams and reality."

Regina recalled Grandpa's confusion in not knowing how much of his dreams were real and how much fantasy. As he kept talking, she wondered whether dreams—imagination—and reality—the surrounding world—could exist simultaneously. There had been many times when Regina talked to someone while imagining something entirely different, or when she daydreamed about wishes she made true in her mind.

Grandpa's agitation snapped her back to him.

"My father said that I wasn't a genius who would find a cure for ALS, that science was intangible, unlike money, which could be counted. Money was real. What could you do with ideas?"

Grandpa muttered, veins popping out of his forehead, "Damn Dad and his money mania, always reproaching and criticizing. What did he know about my reality or my trying to cut a path through the jungle of complexity?"

Regina, unsure how to respond to Grandpa's outburst, asked, "Do you think your father was serious in thinking that science was a game?"

"I don't know," he said. "But it felt like an attack."

Regina thought that Grandpa remembered his past as a mixture of painful truth contaminated with fantasy.

"Well, he was right in a way," Grandpa continued. "I spent a lot of time imagining the existence of Thought-Particles, which have never been identified. Did that idea do anyone any good? Maybe I was a tinkerer imagining my way through life. Maybe. Is that so bad? Why do so many people think in terms of all or none?"

Regina understood how painful that might have been to Grandpa, but yes, Thought-Particles were a product of his imagination.

Grandpa continued to agitate himself and repeated, "What did he know about my reality? What did he risk testing new ideas?"

Regina shook her head, unsure how to respond, surprised to see Grandpa so insecure and afraid to stand by his convictions. The tide had turned from Grandpa supporting her to her supporting him.

"Are ideas less valuable than commodities, like money?" he asked.

Regina didn't answer. She had to think about that question. Are ideas a commodity, she wondered? How are substances connected with ideas? What's the value of ideas without ways to apply them or to make money? Someone must have had the idea of using money to replace trading. Leonardo da Vinci thought about aviation, it was an idea, and he made many drawings of potential flying machines in the 1480s, but he never built one that flew. Were his drawings a waste of time? Maybe. It wasn't until 1903—more than four hundred years later— that the Wright brothers built an airplane that flew. Does the timing of applying an idea affect whether the idea is important as science? Regina's professors at college said that ideas are cheap, and that anyone can think of something outlandish, which doesn't make it science. This raised a wider question for Regina—much more interesting than any one idea: is imagination by itself, without proof (yet), a part of science? She knew that scientists would say, "Of course it is. Imagination is a process that drives scientists." Maybe, she thought, but not all ideas have the same weight. If one is cheap, it doesn't mean all are cheap. Some ideas may hinder science and even be less than cheap by wasting precious time and expense.

As Regina ruminated on all this, Grandpa waited for her answer.

"What do you think, Regina?" he asked again. "Are ideas less valuable than money?"

She couldn't be rushed. "It depends on what you want to buy,

Grandpa, and when you want to buy it. Sorry, I need to think about all this."

"Well, Dad's end wasn't an idea. It was hell," he said, scratching his thighs anxiously.

"You mean when he died?"

"No. Before that. Eventually Dad became quadriplegic, paralyzed from the neck down. He couldn't turn in bed or scratch himself. He couldn't speak or feed himself or write. Only his eyelids could blink. I told him to blink once for 'yes' and twice for 'no' to answer my questions. Our interaction was just my questions and his blinking answers."

Regina, horrified, listened, her mouth slightly open.

"What could be worse?" Grandpa continued. "To be completely enclosed—trapped within and no way out."

Regina wondered if imagination could displace, or at least relieve, such horrible reality if she had witnessed that or, even worse, had ALS herself. She sat at the edge of her chair, rubbed the back of her neck with her hand, and sighed. Could imagination soothe the suffering of an ALS patient? Was it possible for someone to relieve harsh physical reality—suffering and pain—with imagination? How different were reality and imagination?

"Grandpa, did *you* ever imagine that your dad was not suffering as much as you thought he was, to imagine that it might have been less bad for him than it appeared to be, to relieve yourself, if nothing else?" she asked.

"What are you driving at, Regina?"

"I'm curious if imagination could have relieved you from your dad's suffering, or maybe even if his imagination might have helped him endure his suffering, which, of course, you wouldn't be able to know? In other words: can imagination become a type of reality? Sounds far-fetched, I know. I'm just thinking aloud."

"Not as far-fetched as you may think, Regina. I've had similar ideas and kept a diary in which I've jotted down such thoughts, many inspired by my mother. The diary must be somewhere among my things. I'll look for it later."

Diary? Oh, my god. I've got to find it, she thought.

"Your mother, Grandpa? What about her?" she continued. "Apart from her being an actor, you haven't talked about her."

"Dad wasn't my only obstacle during that difficult period," said Grandpa. "Mom imagined obstacles and problems in an entirely different way. I didn't mention that to the journalist, but I never understood how she could do it."

Grandpa told Regina that his mother lived in a swirl of imagination, but not necessarily consciously. She insisted that her ex-husband would get better throughout his illness. "Don't worry, dear. You'll be fine," she told him repeatedly. "You look better today. I bet you will be up and around pretty soon."

"She wasn't lying," Grandpa said. "She meant it. She was in denial."

Regina was struggling to remain calm as she heard about the devastating effect of ALS on Grandpa as well as on his father, and his mother denied it? Was it possible? What did that mean? Denying ALS was delusional, mentally sick … or was it a form of imagination when it trespassed the common reactions of most people? Why did everything need to be labeled and put in a certain file? There's no law that says imagination needs to be conscious, or denial needs to be delusional. Nothing needs to be only one thing. She tried to stay focused on Grandpa's story, but her mind overpowered it.

"Her ridiculous denial was to calm herself," Grandpa added. "It enabled her to endure his illness."

So, thought Regina, the delusion must have been her imagination protecting her, creating a softer world, less threatening, one she could endure. It didn't seem to have much effect on Grandpa's dad, who was a realist in spades. For him, pigs couldn't fly, and rocks couldn't oink. However, he *imagined* what reality would be for a scientist, so obviously not everything was perceived as real for him.

"That must have driven you crazy, Grandpa, seeing your father terminally sick and your mother not accepting it."

"Yeah, but maybe she wouldn't have been like that if I hadn't been there. How would I know? Maybe she imagined that I was suffering more than I might have been and wanted to help me. When Dad died, she did seem at rest. 'It's for the best, dear,' she said to me."

"It's for the best, dear," echoed in Regina's mind in her mom's voice.

"Was your mother always passive, or at least coping, by seeing things how she wanted them to be, Grandpa?"

"No. It was different. In general, she made trivial issues into obstacles greater than they were," he said. "She might have considered seating dinner guests who didn't know each other an obstacle to overcome. She created obstacles from situations that weren't obstacles at all, and then not conquering these imagined obstacles made her feel unworthy in a bland landscape."

Grandpa lowered his voice and gazed into space and looked thoughtful as he mumbled to himself, "I didn't even realize that I too imagined I needed obstacles to overcome to feel successful. What's the accomplishment if success is served on a silver platter without any effort? 'Here's the victory. Congratulations. You can pick up your trophy at your convenience. What an accomplishment! You must be so proud.'

"Sorry. I seem to have gone off on a tangent. Emotions can get tangled. People often laugh or cry in relief from fear, or feel guilty when happy to survive, or ashamed for wanting to defeat a weak opponent or friend. Emotions are one big package filled with contradictions and surprises. I wonder how often they're casualties of imagination.

"Let's have a snack for dinner and I'll tell you about absurdity."

Chapter 9

"THE JOURNALIST KEPT pressing me for what I consider gossip," Grandpa said after dinner. "I told her I was a laboratory recluse and didn't do much networking, where gripes and gossip abound. I was getting fed up with this so-called interview, but she didn't let me off that easily. I worried that she might want me to make something up and stretch reality. Absurd, wouldn't you say? What did I know? I told her what I remembered Bethesda was like and about the frustration of bureaucracy, which any large establishment needs to deal with. Maybe she could spin something relevant to the Obliteration, although I seriously doubted that."

Absurd? Regina liked the sound of that. Just the idea of absurd made her want to write a short story. She prepared herself to hear the last installment of this saga, which she had already entitled in her mind, *The Mysterious Topsy-Turvy Tragedy of the Obliteration: Triumph of Ambiguities and Absurdities.*

Grandpa appeared to be drifting off to some private island. After a moment, he looked at Regina and said, "Funny about that."

"Funny about what?"

"About knowing I was stretching credibility, yet willing to do exactly that. I had the same feeling when I wrote my Thought-Particles article. Ricardo, well his ghost, told me that he knew what I was feeling, since it was true for him too when he speculated about jellyfish seeing evolution. He knew some of his speculations were stretching what he imagined, but he believed his speculations were true, so why not put them out there as speculations, which he supported with some evidence? Neither Ricardo nor I ever claimed that our ideas were proved. Isn't science as much about ideas to follow than proofs to obtain?"

Ricardo? Regina wanted to know about Grandpa.

"Credibility is overrated, Regina," he said. "Credibility is fickle and, as the journalist might say, 'soft,' on the edge of truth and nonsense. However, ideas remain, no matter what happens to them, whether proved or debunked. Even if forgotten for some time, they will come back to haunt you. Once you put an idea out there, you own it. It lives forever. The best you can do is modify it. If people don't believe in ideas, why would they vilify you if you have them?"

He paused. "Anyway, I believe that Thought-Particles are sure as hell significant, even if no one has seen any yet. No one knows who caused the Obliteration, but nobody doubts that it happened. Someone did it. Fuck credibility! The Obliteration happened although no one knows who did it."

Regina felt pushed over by gusts of wind blowing in every direction.

Grandpa settled down from his agitated detours, and he said that the journalist thought emotions were important and he might give her something to chew on.

Grandpa continued. "The journalist said depression sometimes leads to suicide, and a manic state can result in pointless destruction, and bizarre behavior—and the Obliteration was bizarre—can often be traced to out-of-control emotional states or mental illness. I didn't disagree with any of that, so she asked me about the emotional climate before the Obliteration. Were people discouraged or acting bizarrely? Did anything like that strike me at the time, or now?

"I told her I didn't remember the atmosphere being extreme one way or the other. Rather, it was level, with no peaks of passion, or over-the-top political demonstrations. There were no signs of anarchy with riots and looting. There seemed to be fewer indiscriminate shootings and homicides before the Obliteration, but I didn't have any statistics. She would have to look those up if she thought they were relevant."

Alarm bells went off in Regina's mind when he reminded her that the journalist was recording everything he said. She was scared to ask him what else he'd said, but Grandpa seemed to sense that and immediately cooled down from specifics that could come back to hurt him to generalities that had little bite.

"The journalist didn't respond when I told her life seemed boring at the time of the Obliteration. Cars were gray and fashions were stagnant, there was little interest in sports."

Regina noted that Grandpa's engagement also ran downhill as he spoke. Was it really the epoch that lacked peaks and valleys, or was it just him? She knew he had been depressed and frustrated, very much so, when his colleagues didn't think much of his Thought-Particles. Was he looking at everything through that tainted lens?

"You've never told me about any of this before."

He shrugged his shoulders. "Progress was mostly in technology—a barrage of dispassionate electronics and smaller computer chips with faster reactions. Science benefited, but what about the privilege of being alive? The collective mood had no accents. The world was sinking. Am I making sense?"

"I think so," Regina said, although she wasn't sure he was.

"The journalist persisted in looking for absolutely anything that might have foreshadowed the Obliteration. I felt more attacked than questioned, even though she didn't know anything about me to attack, or about Thought-Particles, or … oh, forget it."

Why didn't he tell the journalist once and for all that he had no clues for her to follow up and just quit? Regina became increasingly infuriated and worried.

"There were rules at the Vision Science Center that were frustrating, to say the least," he told her, getting more agitated. "The government limited socializing with superiors or senior officials in industry, had complicated travel rules that meant scientists often couldn't attend important meetings for their research, and buying equipment needed pages of justification. All this bureaucracy was intended to be transparent, honest, fair to the taxpayers, who supported us. I have no qualms about that. But where was judgment? So much was about appearance. I felt, and I know some of my colleagues felt, that we had to continually prove we were innocent. That didn't help anyone's morale. However, it was easier to follow the rules than to fight the system. So, I guess, I told the journalist about a boring world lined with frustrations. However, I also told her how grateful I was for all the support I received to do my research. What can I say? Frustrations are built into the structure of our lives.

"However, come to think about it, the apathy mixed with frustration might drive someone to sabotage. There is a history of that," he said.

Grandpa started to speak faster.

"I'm not exaggerating! There were times I couldn't stand it."

Regina wondered whether the journalist could stand it either. Again she wondered if Grandpa was losing it. She crossed her fingers, as if a helping spirit might protect him from the journalist, whom she didn't trust.

Grandpa brought imagination into the story again.

"There's more, Regina, which you'll appreciate as a storyteller. The world at the time of the Obliteration was a fictional reality. Nothing seemed real, and I think Thought-Particles got caught in the web. When nothing seems real, imagination distorts what you think you know and see. Do you agree?"

Yes, she agreed. Imagination did seem like the foil to reality.

"But what I'm saying is not imagination, Regina. I felt my integrity was challenged. Did they think my Thought-Particles theory was a lie? That would be absurd. Ricardo had the same reaction that I had when I told him there were times that I felt I was in a prison of restrictions to appear innocent."

"Still, Grandpa, aren't you being a bit dramatic about the role of bureaucratic regulations and whether things were dull, as occurs from time to time in every society?"

"Regulations aren't drama. Bureaucracy isn't harmless. Boredom leaves time and space for imagination to fill. All it takes is a few, maybe only one despot or bored person with gripes, to destroy almost anything, including blowing up the medical center, if only to show the world how he feels and who he imagines he is. I believe that some of the scientists felt that way—very frustrated—at the time of the Obliteration. Committees were formed by the scientists for strategizing how to deal with all the frustrations. Yes, it felt like a perfect storm was approaching, and then the Obliteration, one huge explosion. I'm beginning to convince myself of the dangers of the time, dangers I didn't take seriously enough. What do you think, Ricardo?"

Ricardo again? She wondered whether he would say that the Obliteration was caused by Thought-Particles or by Ricardo's jellyfish!

"Do you hear me, Ricardo?" he said. "He doesn't come to see me anymore or even answer me. What a disappointment."

Regina didn't know what to think. Regulation, frustration, and boredom causing the Obliteration? Thought-Particles contaminating reality and jellyfish seeing evolution? Grandpa still imagining he's talking to Ricardo as his friend?

He finally returned to the journalist.

"The journalist looked me in the eye and asked me whether frustrating bureaucratic regulations, even if lacking in judgment at times but not meaning to oppress, in a bland boring world outside of work, would make me, or anyone, want to blow up the place. My answer was no, it made me want to change the rules and read a good book. But, I said, someone else might get sufficiently angry or frustrated to be driven to sabotage. Who knows what people think or imagine or … explode one way or another?"

Yes, Regina thought. Far-fetched, but living under frustrating rules with no escape might feel like being in prison, gathering anger that foreshadowed sabotage such as the Obliteration, especially for a mentally unbalanced person. Still, she thought, was Grandpa drifting from partial reality to let his imagination flow? He loved good stories as much as she did. On the other hand, could he have fused his memories with his imagination to create an apparent reality?

"What are you thinking, Regina? You're very quiet."

She paused before answering. "There's a lot to think about. You do torture yourself a bit, don't you?"

"Torture myself? Maybe. I imagine I do, sometimes."

Chapter 10

Regina understood Grandpa's frustrations and his age no doubt didn't help keep his memories straight. He seemed buried under unresolved issues from a long time ago and had become mixed with his fanciful imagination to which he added a drop or two of reality.

But it was the journalist she worried about. Would she make him seem unhinged to bring attention to the Obliteration to advance her career? There was no way to predict how she would react to the barrage of information, much disconnected, which Grandpa had fed her. Presumably, she would fact-check what she could, such as possible documentary movies or articles to see if anything could have accounted for his wild dreams. Also, it would be easy for her to look up past administrative regulations at the Vision Science Center that might have been as frustrating as Grandpa talked about. Hopefully, she would understand that a ninety-year-old might not be the most reliable source. Oh, why had she pushed Grandpa to accept the interview? In retrospect, it didn't make much sense. Nonetheless, she might be blowing it out of proportion—hopefully—and overly pessimistic. Maybe she unduly feared the journalist, and the whole matter would fade away. But what if it didn't?

If it didn't fade and the journalist wrote a disparaging article, there was little Regina or anyone else could do about it. What was more important now was for her to try and understand Grandpa, and that also meant understanding Ricardo, since they were a "team" to some extent, at least in Grandpa's mind. She wanted to learn more about Thought-Particles and about Ricardo. Both had theories dependent on imagination that they believed to be true. She would read their original work.

Grandpa

REGINA WAS IMPRESSED by how directly Grandpa had introduced Thought-Particles in his original article. He admitted the major contribution was imagining an abstraction—a thought—as a substance, which alone was a revolutionary idea, simply stated. Great care was given to avoid saying all thoughts or exchanges of ideas involved Thought-Particles. In other words, he was aware of the distinction between imagination and what others accepted as reality. He wrote: "*Thought-Particles did not obviate other mechanisms for acquiring and transferring thoughts.*" He only speculated that Thought-Particles existed, not that they accounted entirely for the complexity of thought. Regina found his last sentence especially interesting: "*It has occurred to me that Thought-Particles suggest profound implications for free-will and social interactions.*"

Regina wondered if Grandpa considered Thought-Particles might be connected to the Obliteration. If so, did that imply in his mind—his imagination—that the Obliteration was a conspiracy by several people being infected with the same Thought-Particles? It would explain his bringing up Thought-Particles when the journalist asked him what he thought might have caused the Obliteration. Grandpa would not have been unhinged, just unclear, probably even in his mind.

Regina also read about how Grandpa's article was received by scientists, which was what had discouraged him so much. Some scientists did find Thought-Particles an interesting hypothesis that shouldn't be dismissed simply because such a particle hadn't been identified yet. What was a particle? Possibly, some scientists said, that thoughts, like photons for light and electrons in atoms, exhibited a wave-particle duality, suggesting that, depending on experimental conditions, a

Thought-Particle could exist both as a particle at a designated position and as a wave which covered a distance. She recalled from her physics classes an astounding phenomenon called entanglement, which stated that separated particles could be perfectly correlated at a distance. If one particle moved in a specific direction, the other unlinked particle did the same. Could Thought-Particles be entangled in some fashion as a form of cooperation between them? This was all beyond what she knew about, and she wasn't sure exactly what she meant.

Could Grandpa be justified in believing in some sort of Thought-Particles, perhaps as a wave-particle duality or entanglement? Was it possible that dreams also have wave properties or some variation of entanglement correlating the sleeping brain with something in the environment? It seemed to her that there was a lot not yet understood. Could these phenomena somehow relate to Grandpa's dreams and touch on a type of reality?

What about Ricardo, the wizard scientist who claimed jellyfish had a brain and were able to see evolution?

Ricardo

RICARDO'S ORIGINAL ARTICLE was published in a popular lay magazine, *Observation and Discovery*, which was out of print, but she found a copy in the archives of the Library of Congress. What jumped out immediately was that the conclusions were carefully qualified as speculations, not proven facts. Ricardo's speculations were based on physical similarities between fixed specimens of different invertebrates in the laboratory and abstract computer images generated from jellyfish eyes linked to their nerve network impaled with electrodes. The speculations were, in Regina's opinion, a result of brilliant observations, and a few scientists had found it worthy of further study. Thus, Ricardo, like Grandpa a century later, had proposed a novel, potentially ground-breaking concept, based on evidence. Yet, it was dismissed as quackery because definitive proof was still lacking. There was also no proof that the ideas couldn't hold some truth. A court trial had convicted Ricardo of irresponsibly wasting government funds on irrelevant research during a depressed economic era. She thought that being jailed for this basic research was reminiscent of so-called witches being burned for virtually no rational reason.

Regina was incensed.

What captured her interest was how Ricardo's speculations led to far-reaching ideas for advancing science, such as investigations on diverse ways for expressing DNA unrelated to the conventional synthesis of RNA. Ricardo had pointed that out at his trial, when he said, "*Imagine also if we discovered how jellyfish store and retrieve memories of evolution: we might be able to learn how to download information into our own brains like information is downloaded into a computer. Putting all sorts of information into our brains would become quick and easy. Who knows, we might even be able to link our brain with an animal's brain and see the world as it does. The practical ramifications of my jellyfish research are potentially huge!*"

Regina was flooded with new feelings. First, innovative hypotheses, even before proof, had an essential role in stimulating advances in science. Reading the Ricardo and Grandpa's articles gave Regina renewed pride in her scientific lineage, not only for their intelligence, but also for their courage to persist. Mixed with pride was fierce anger, even more than anger—rage! How could the world be so stupid, have such limited insight, and be so mean, yes, *mean*, to put someone with novel ideas in prison, or ridicule a scientist for important concepts because they hadn't yet been proved? It was OUTRAGEOUS! She wouldn't stand for it, not now, not ever. Her choice of career wasn't between writing or science anymore. It would be science. She would redeem Ricardo and Grandpa from their unfair status as failures, and even elevate them to the visionaries that, in her opinion, they were. She would not only make discoveries herself in science, but she would also widen the scope of how science was appreciated. Yes. She would. Queen Regina. She would make science her court and reign with honor.

—⁂—

SHE TOLD GRANDPA the next day that she had read his articles on Thought-Particles, then those of Ricardo on jellyfish. "They were great,

Grandpa. What clever and exciting ideas you both had. You should have a trophy on your mantle instead of the broken brick you saved from the Obliteration."

Grandpa smiled, which Regina interpreted as him thinking she had a lot to learn about life and what the world was like.

"At least I didn't land in jail, as Ricardo did."

That wasn't sufficient compensation, she thought.

"You need more, Grandpa. So does Ricardo, even though he's dead, or an apparition. I'm going to erase the blemish of Ricardo's felony conviction and the lack of appreciation for your Thought-Particles theory. I will. You can count on it."

Grandpa remained calm.

"It's not only for Ricardo and you that I want to change history—do you think I'm going overboard? Don't answer that because it doesn't matter. I'm selfish too. I don't want such injustices to weigh on my life as a scientist. We should be proud of the Sztein/Resin/Resin lineage of visionary scientists. The question isn't *whether* I can do that. It's *how* will I do it? How to resurrect legacies and place them on a pedestal in plain sight? I'll need a relevant discovery that changes the way science is viewed, by scientists, laymen and history. Wish me luck!"

Grandpa took her hand gently, stroked her cheek, and then kissed it. "Thanks, Regina, my Queen Regina. I have no doubts that you will reign with wisdom and dignity."

Regina called it a day. It was time to go home and relax.

Chapter 11

REGINA HAD JUST gotten up the next day when the phone rang. Grandpa was hysterical and, on a rampage, spouting more expletives than she had ever heard come out of his mouth.

"That fucking journalist, and the spineless newspaper too, for publishing her nonsense. As for the readers—ignoramuses, all of them. It's a miracle they can read … they don't realize how damaging, cruel, false, tragically misleading the news is these days. Such fake news isn't meant to misinform, which, of course, it does. It's meant to incite a war against science, against reason, against … against … me! She even mentions you, that bitch journalist, with her cutesy tan skirt and shirt covered with question marks. All she does is ask questions since she doesn't have an answer to anything. Some journalist! At least, she considers you neutral, a nurse-like granddaughter who tries her best to limit her delusional grandfather. She doesn't even call me *Dr.* Roger Resin. That journalist has no interest in reporting the news or writing meaningful editorials or figuring out what caused the Obliteration. She likes the nuclear option! Sure. So would every dictator and despot who ever lived. She wants to destroy as much as she can as quickly as possible. That's why she's so fixated on the Obliteration. She loves it. She wants to have another one. That's why she wants to know how they, whoever they are, did it. Shit. Damn. Fuck. She wants another Obliteration."

"Nice speech, Grandpa. I've never heard you more eloquent. But take it easy. I haven't read anything yet. Maybe you should be flattered that she thinks you're worth a nuclear option. Whatever she said isn't worth a heart attack. Get the coffee ready, but don't burn yourself by spilling it in a nervous frenzy. I'm on my way."

Chapter 12

T HE JOURNALIST'S ARTICLE was in Grandpa's outstretched hands. "Read it, Regina, and let me know what you think. This is more than atrocious, it's …"

"Okay, Grandpa, I get it. Maybe it's not as bad as you think. Don't exaggerate. I'll read it slowly aloud. It may sound different, less damning, coming from me. I'll skim the parts that repeat what we both know you told her, okay? I don't want you to go ballistic again. It's her interpretation that we need to focus on."

"Sure, sure. Go ahead. What a bitch! Not you. Her." Grandpa was livid and he was scratching his thighs so energetically that Regina feared it would cause bleeding.

The Obliteration—the massive explosion—of the science research center thirty years ago in the heart of Bethesda was devastating, killing more than five hundred scientists, and injuring three times as many. Some sociologists considered the Obliteration the straw of discontent that broke modern civilization as we knew it then. Optimism and growth fell to pessimism and mediocrity. Social interactions became …

"Yada, yada, yada, Grandpa. I'll skip down to what pisses you off so much."

In view of the Obliteration being a pivotal sea-change, like the catastrophe known as 9/11 at the beginning of the twenty-first century, it was, and still is, essential to determine what caused it, who was responsible, and how to prevent such damage in the future. It's a matter of national security. Surprisingly, everything about it has remained mysterious. Even stranger, no one has investigated it in the last twenty years, despite its unknown cause. Is there a cover-up still going on? The Obliteration has moved from social, or perhaps political, terrorism to historical enigma, and there it lies fallow, waiting to be repeated. This journalist decided to reactivate interest in the tragedy, hoping finally to solve the case.

There are fewer than a handful of Obliteration survivors. One of the few, Roger Resin, ninety, a minor scientist at the second or third level of significance with dubious credibility, was seriously injured, recovered, and retired immediately after the explosion. He had this to say when recently interviewed: "It was quite an event. I have it from trustworthy sources that the Obliteration was performed by terrorists in a truck delivering desks filled with explosives, and by pedestrians belonging to an unknown cult distinguished by an igloo neck tattoo, who filtered into the campus with briefcases filled with explosives. The truck was chased down and the two terrorists killed by police, so no information was obtained from them."

The igloo cult members, according to Mr. Resin, "coordinated the sabotage by planting the explosives in the buildings and creating gas leaks, which intensified the explosion." Mr. Resin ended the interview by saying, "The Obliteration was a dramatic, well-coordinated act fit for a movie, and it was, in fact, described in part in several documentaries."

Fact-checking found no evidence for any of these causes or for the documentary movies. There was, however, a gas leak discovered in one of the many pipes much too small to have caused any harm. Mr. Resin, clearly struggling with cognitive issues, relied on his granddaughter, Regina Resin, a college graduate who prides herself on writing fiction, for support. It is imperative that more reliable information is obtained before it is too late. Time is a common graveyard.

As a matter of note, Mr. Resin's late relative from the twentieth century, Ricardo Sztein, was also a scientist at the Vision Science Center in its early days. He was convicted of irresponsible spending of government funds for irrelevant research, claiming that jellyfish can see evolution. That might make a more likely box office hit movie than Mr. Resin's fantasies.

Regina was trembling when she finished reading the blasphemous article. She was speechless, as was Grandpa.

"My god …"

"I know," said Grandpa.

"What will Mom and Dad think?"

"What will anyone think?"

"We need to sue her," said Grandpa. "See what I mean? A bitch—a lying, cruel bitch."

"You're right, about the bitch part. But I'm not sure you're right about a lawsuit, not yet anyway. Do you know how much it would cost, and how much it would spread the lies far more than they are now? No one is really going to care or remember what the journalist wrote. And you did tell her about your dreams. I feel terrible about writing that story."

"Well, what then? Do nothing? Go hide in Antarctica?"

"That place is too cold."

"So, what …?"

"Do you know what scares me?" said Regina. "That she video recorded everything. What if she posts it online, or, oh my god, it goes viral!"

Grandpa's face turned vomit green. "It better not," he said, somewhat desperately.

"Remember I told you the other day that I was going to become a scientist and clear our whole family from a type of infamy. I meant it, and now I mean it more than ever." Regina had never looked more determined.

The phone rang and Grandpa picked up. It was Regina's dad.

"I can't believe what you've done, Dad!" he shouted into the phone. "You've ruined our family, my daughter, your granddaughter, all of us. Damn you and your meaningless Thought-Particles."

"Can I speak to Regina's mom, please?" Grandpa said, very calmly considering his state.

"No. She's too upset to speak to you, and furious with Regina. What's wrong with the two of you?"

He slammed the phone down before Grandpa had a chance to respond.

"I didn't lie about my dreams and their possible link to the Obliteration. What I said was true. It was based on information that I had received. I know it. I didn't make anything up. But it was so long ago. I can't remember exactly seeing a movie or where I got all my information. I could almost visualize what I said, but … it was also a blur. I realize that. I remember writing something about it in my diary, which I kept then. But I've lost the diary. I've looked everywhere but can't find it. Maybe it will turn up someplace. Oh, Regina, I'm sorry. I hate being old."

The diary again. She had to find it.

Regina suggested that they cool off and meet tomorrow to think about whether there was anything they could do.

Chapter 13

REGINA WENT FOR a long walk and stopped for fast food. She hoped that the journalist's article would be ignored or forgotten as she ignored or forgot the news of whatever had nothing to do with her. After lunch, she needed to simmer down more and went for another walk on her favorite path in the nearby woods. Living in rural Elizabethtown had its benefits. She loved the place.

Her parents were having a heated conversation about the newspaper article when she got home. Her father glared at her when she came in. Before they had a chance to say anything to her, she said in a deadpan voice, "Never mind about me for dinner. I've eaten. Sorry you're so upset because of a pack of lies told by a journalist more interested in her career than the truth."

She knew, however, that as cruel and misleading as the article was, it did hold fragments of truth. So little was known about the Obliteration that almost anything said or guessed was a possibility.

Regina went to her bedroom, fought despair, and tried to convince herself that there had been articles more damaging than this one, and the smeared subjects usually survived the damage. It will be soon forgotten, she thought. The hell with it. Of course, none of that did any good. She remained miserable. Why, oh why did she write the story that Grandpa had given to the journalist? Why did she coax Grandpa to be interviewed? Going to the graduation was hard enough on him.

She didn't take his age seriously enough. Did she accompany him to Bethesda so that some of that imagined glamour would rub off on her? She wondered exactly why the journalist had even considered him for the interview, especially in view of his age. He wasn't that reliable anymore.

She laid down on her bed, with no plans to budge from there. She had no appetite and didn't want dinner. She wasn't going to talk to her parents. She fell asleep within minutes of closing her eyes.

She saw herself and the arrogant face of the journalist in a dream, and she told her in a cold voice, "Grandpa's dead, thanks to you, bitch!"

The journalist had no reaction. She didn't even look surprised. Instead of anger, she said, "He was dead before I even met him." Then she added, "He was such a gentleman, your grandfather, and so intelligent. I liked him, but I couldn't verify most of what he told me when I fact-checked what I could. That's necessary for any article I write. You must understand that."

The journalist's appearance suddenly changed from a lovely young woman to a vicious warrior exposing white fangs, from angel to devil, and then back again, back and forth.

"I couldn't find the documentary movies he told me about concerning the Obliteration," the journalist continued, now an angel with a pleasing voice. "I wonder where Dr. Resin got his interesting stories," she asked, smiling. She called him Dr. in the dream.

In an instant, her face appeared ferocious again. "He's a liar, a bad man," she said, in a deeper, gruff voice. "I'll kill him. It's my job, then I'll climb up on his dead body and smother whatever may be left alive."

She disappeared, and flashing images of trucks, desks, igloos, and tattoos floating in space appeared. These images changed to ones of open books and movie reels and spectators in a theater. The audience gasped when an image of an old, shriveled man with ALS appeared, but within seconds his image was replaced by a body thrown out of a crashing car.

The journalist again entered, this time only her face, still alternating between ferocious and peaceful. Occasionally, the vicious face screamed, "Liar!" and then the serious face followed and said as a matter of fact, "Truth." Nothing else. Just "Truth."

Regina woke up, startled, raised her head, and looked around, thankful that this was only a dream. She placed her head back on the pillow, fell asleep again, and the dream resumed.

Newspaper headlines appeared in bold letters: *Fake News Topples Liar.*

The journalist returned, laughing, then serious. "Truth always wins because it's true," she said in a somber, judicial voice. "I'm obliged to report it."

Regina stirred, turning one way and then another in an attempt to make herself comfortable.

Grandpa appeared with his eyes soaked in tears. Blood spilled out of his mouth. He said, his words garbled, "I don't lie."

Regina put her arms around him. "It's okay, Grandpa," she said. "Every truth is a lie for someone, and no lies are devoid of truth. I'll protect you."

The journalist appeared again, repeating. "Delusional … delusional … delusional …"

"Delusional?" said Grandpa, who suddenly displaced the journalist and looked younger and angry. He laughed.

Grandpa's laugh woke Regina up. It was morning and she was angry and anxious.

Truth always wins, she thought. But what's the truth?

Chapter 14

REGINA WENT TO see Grandpa in the morning. He looked shell-shocked. She thought that the article saying he was a minor, insignificant scientist (was the journalist kidding?), and of dubious credibility (really?), was what most affected him. Without that he would have been angry but not destroyed. At least, she thought, the journalist didn't bring up his Thought-Particles theory and ridicule it.

Seeing Grandpa in such a state solidified her determination to become a scientist and prove the journalist wrong. Ricardo and Grandpa were important and innovative scientists, the "shoulders" upon which later generations of scientists stand. She wanted to redeem them. That was her long-term goal. She considered it a mission.

He brought up Thought-Particles shortly after she arrived. "The journalist couldn't have said that Thought-Particles were third-tier science, like she called me. She doesn't even know about them and certainly wouldn't understand how important the idea is. She's no scientist. She's an ambitious opportunist, hardly even a journalist, otherwise she would have thrown in the Thought-Particles for good measure."

He scratched his thighs.

He's right about that, Regina said to herself.

Grandpa's expression suddenly dropped. His eyes appeared to lose focus; his mind seemed detached. The fear on his face wasn't there anymore. His anger transformed into indifference, resignation, as if the battle was lost, no longer important. The journalist had won. Time seemed suspended. Regina imagined Grandpa's face in red, which turned blue, then pale green, soft yellow, and finally colorless. No, it wasn't her imagination. He was getting paler and paler.

Something had happened, something serious, she thought, but then he said, "I believe science is a narrative of some kind—observations, facts linked by educated guesses, speculations—a narrative that shifts with every new observation. Thought-Particles are part of the narrative."

These thoughts were coherent and vintage Grandpa, yet he no longer sounded like himself.

"Ricardo, are you here? Good. I'm glad you finally came to see me," he said. "Why have you been gone for all these years since I retired? I was hurt. Ah, I see you're wearing orange socks. This must be a special occasion. Well, it's special for me to have you visit me again. Regina, say hi to Ricardo."

This was beyond weird; it was scary. Was Grandpa having a stroke, or something else? Yet she humored him. "Hi, Ricardo."

Grandpa then shifted back to whatever he was trying to say and ignored Ricardo.

"Isolated observations aren't science until they're linked into a logical story, true for the moment, but not forever, so the narratives are at least part imagination," he continued.

He had told her the same thing many times. Had he forgotten that? No, he was just rambling again.

"Everything changes eventually," he said. "Our interpretations of nature are as lame as a puppet dubbed with a voice by a ventriloquist. The puppet's voice is not its own. Hmmmm ... I never thought of it like that before. You bring out new ideas in me, Regina. An interesting idea, don't you think?

"We scientists see nature as mindless puppets controlled by ventriloquists. And who are the ventriloquists? Journalists! Sorry, I'm rambling again, old guy that I am.

"God, I'm so proud of you, Regina. You're so smart, but you also have such a great imagination. That's important, you know. Imagination is a thing by itself. It determines one's life."

Grandpa's acknowledgment triggered an avalanche of ambition in her, but also insecurity. Did he say that imagination determines life? Look what it did to him and to Ricardo. That wasn't such a happy determination.

"Thanks, Grandpa," she said. "I do have imagination," she admitted. "Like you. Sometimes my imagination drives me nuts, because I know that many of my thoughts, maybe most of them, are silly, even ridiculous. Probably all I do is twist them into pretzels. Do you know what I mean?"

He nodded. "With how much salt?"

"A lot. Do you know that salt was more precious than money a long time ago?"

She was trying to change the topic with a bit of levity.

"I did know that," he said, sighing with resignation.

His eyelids lowered, leaving only a crack of space for vision, and through that crack she saw that the fire in his eyes had faded to embers. Was he okay? Was he bored? Did he want her to leave? The article must have exhausted him. She wasn't sure. It was still the morning. But Grandpa was ninety. Did she expect him to be training to run a marathon?

"Are you feeling okay, Grandpa? Do you want me to go so you can rest?"

He looked up and half-smiled. "I'm okay," he said, not much louder than a whisper. "It's just age."

"Let me know if you want me to go," she said again. She wanted to stay and was being selfish.

She stayed, and then said she felt her overly active imagination pounded her brain like ocean waves crashing on rocks along the shore during a storm. She thought imagination was critical for the arts and literature, and maybe for philosophy, but for science? She had reservations. Nature's imagination had nothing to do with *her* imagination. She couldn't take credit for what nature had dreamed up. She had to be careful how she used her imagination as a scientist. Ricardo's imagination landed him in jail. Grandpa's imaginative Thought-Particles dangled without scientific recognition. At least he wasn't imprisoned for the concept, as he had acknowledged. She wondered whether Thought-Particles, as innovative as they were, was a scientific achievement. Was imagination alone an accomplishment in science, or in any field for that matter, or were only proven facts or tangible products, like making money or producing something or winning competitions, accomplishments?

She pondered these thoughts to herself. She closed her eyes as if to hide.

Grandpa said nothing. He didn't even grunt. She opened her eyes and … what!? His body was slouched, his head drooping over his chest. He was limp. Coffee mixed with brown saliva dribbled down his chin.

"Grandpa!" she said, her voice hysterical. She shook his arm. "Wake up! What's the matter? Do you hear me?"

"Whaaat?" he answered, dazed. He lifted his head a few inches. "Yes … of course … love you, Regina … where am I? Oh, oh … my head. It hurts." He clutched the back of his head, his face contorted into an ugly grimace.

"G-g-good-b-bye," he stuttered, which she had never heard him do before. "Goodbye," he repeated more clearly, trying to smile, unsuccessfully, as if nothing mattered anymore, not even what the journalist wrote. He wasn't Grandpa anymore.

Regina raised his limp hand and kissed it, over and over, until it was wet with her tears. Her left eyelid fluttered like never before. She cried and cried and cried for longer than she could remember ever crying in the past. She had no idea how long she sat there, with his lifeless hand in her grip.

"Goodbye, Grandpa. I love you. Goodbye."

—⧓—

SHE CALLED THE emergency line to report Grandpa's death and to request an ambulance to take away his body. She didn't call her parents to tell them Grandpa was dead yet and stayed with his corpse until the ambulance came. She kissed his forehead. His skin felt cold on her lips, as lifeless as leather. Her voice was stronger now, her eyes drier.

"Thank you, Grandpa."

She let the moment linger, and then she poured herself another cup of coffee as her "last supper," so she gave him a cup too. She might drink his after she had finished her own, a way to join him briefly for the last time.

She sipped her coffee slowly to make it last. There was no reason to rush. She felt her life collapsing as she accepted the hard reality that life would never be the same again for her. She imagined a disintegrating structure—an indescribable image.

Grandpa seemed so happy when Ricardo made his final entrance. Did he have a premonition to see Ricardo, his ghost, or apparition, or hallucination, or whatever Grandpa called him, a final time while he was alive before he joined him for eternity?

They had talked to one another, shared experiences, strategized about careers, and felt the same apprehensions and disappointments without having to explain or dwell on them. They understood each other. Ricardo enlarged Grandpa into two people for the price of one. What an enrichment! What good fortune! Yes, together they were one, Grandpa had said, and even felt proud to have given birth to a new and different Ricardo. Imagination. Was there anything more important?

Would they have been close friends and colleagues if they had been alive at the same time? The questions that can't be answered aren't necessarily the most important, but they're the ones that remain.

Was it a mistake for Grandpa to live with an imagined Ricardo? Was it delusional, as the journalist repeatedly said in Regina's dream? No, she thought. Grandpa had said that mistakes from one perspective aren't necessarily mistakes from another perspective. Was it a mistake for Ricardo to indulge his imagination and escape to the mangrove swamps of Puerto Rico to study jellyfish and then imagine that they see evolution? No again. That became a highlight of his scientific life. Wasn't that important? Ricardo's speculations were thought-provoking uses of imagination that had the potential to make a sea-change in science. It was a question of perspective.

Regina wondered whether Grandpa might become her invisible

partner, friend, confidant, ghost, apparition, guru, staunch supporter, protector—perhaps all of these—whatever Ricardo had been to Roger. Did she even want that? No, she wasn't Grandpa, she didn't have his imagination. She had her own. She also knew that she couldn't—wouldn't—share herself with anyone, even with Grandpa. She was Regina—Queen Regina, as Grandpa called her—the one and only, royalty to reckon with in an anti-aristocratic world.

"What do you think about that, Grandpa?" she asked the corpse. "I love you, you know that, and I'll never forget you. Never. But we are different people. We need our individuality. At least I need mine. Do you agree? And you have yours, especially now."

Silence.

"Grandpa, can you hear me?" she said aloud. "Give me a sign if you do? Make something drop or send a Thought-Particle in my direction."

Nothing dropped. No Thought-Particle arrived. Grandpa didn't budge.

The ambulance arrived to take away the body, and she went home.

Chapter 15

GRANDPA'S DEATH RELEASED the tension created by the journalist's article, which died with Grandpa in Regina's mind. Regina didn't talk about Grandpa, but she didn't stop thinking about him. Her goals were clear. She would go to graduate school, get a Ph.D. in science and, ultimately, resurrect the legacies and honor of Grandpa and Ricardo and make her scientific lineage proud. That didn't mean she wouldn't distinguish herself from them. Queen Regina had big plans.

First, Grandpa's small estate needed to be tended. Dad, Grandpa's son, would help her, of course, while Mom would pretend to mourn. She suddenly decided that Grandpa was a wonderful man, a father-in-law like no other. How lucky she had been! "He was such a dear man. We loved him so," she said. While Dad could be helpful in settling Grandpa's estate, she had been designated the executor of the will, and she would take care of whatever needed to be done—burial, legal matters, announcements. Grandpa had requested there be no memorial. He had purchased a cemetery plot next to Robin.

Grandpa's Will gave Regina all his money, which was minimal, and his possessions, which she had no use for. What mattered for her was that he had given of himself when he was alive. That was the most valuable gift she could have asked for. She sold his Persian rug, a few old science books, and the antique Amish chairs, and gave away his clothes, kitchen utensils, dilapidated furniture, outdated computer, and other knick-knacks to a local charity.

Regina went with Dad for a final check that the house was ready to be sold. They had done a thorough job. Regina felt a pit of emptiness in her gut that matched the emptiness of the house when they entered, but she kept that feeling to herself. Before leaving, she noticed a shadow coming from the glass shelf at the top of a kitchen cabinet. She asked Dad if he could reach whatever it was, since it was too high for her and there was nothing left to stand on. He stretched on his tiptoes and retrieved a small notebook, which he handed to her, saying, "What do you think this is, Regina?"

There was nothing written on the worn cover. When she opened it, however, she read *Notes of Interest: 2152–2187*. Her eyes suddenly lit up with flames of excitement.

"Oh, my god. I can't believe this. It's incredible," she said.

"What is it?" Dad asked, sensing its importance.

"This changes everything, Dad."

"What do you mean? What's changed? What's 'everything'?"

"That's what I want to know. It's Grandpa's diary from when he was thirty-two to sixty-seven years old. It must have something about the Obliteration, his dreams maybe, whatever he was talking about to the journalist. I don't know."

"Can you even read it, Regina? It's so faded, and the writing is so tiny. How did he even write that small?"

She was wondering that herself, but she would use a magnifying glass if necessary. With overflowing curiosity, she told Dad she had to go home and try to read it right away. There was nothing more they could do at the house. They drove home, with her clutching the notebook as if it were the Dead Sea Scrolls.

REGINA SPENT THE entire afternoon glued to that small black notebook. Dad had been right that it was hard to read the tiny scribble, but she could decipher most of it. She wondered if Grandpa had kept other diaries or any other writings that might have included information about the Obliteration that she had missed seeing when she cleared the house. It didn't matter. She had this treasure in his handwriting, and she extracted whatever she could from it.

Much of it was mundane idle thoughts, experiments that didn't work, a few that did, and bits of gossip. Regina was surprised that he took the trouble to include the gossip in his diary. He had never told her any gossip or indicated that he had been interested in any she might have heard. The diary expressed his interest in writing, which resonated with the bond she felt with him about literature. He stressed imagination, how important that was for a writer, and how fiction and truth often felt like the same thing for him. That too resonated with her. He also questioned the importance of imagination in science, as she had, if whatever was imagined had not been proved yet. Regina wondered if he was thinking about Thought-Particles when he wrote that. She was thinking about more than Thought-Particles.

She turned the wrinkled page with its browned, aged edges and— eureka! Several pages were devoted to the Obliteration. Her heart beat faster. "Yes," she said aloud. "Finally."

Grandpa wrote that section after he had recovered from his injuries, and he mentioned that he planned on retiring in Elizabethtown, where his son and family lived. I was only five then, she thought. He complained of pain in his left shoulder, which he hoped would eventually go away. She knew that it never disappeared completely. He wrote that he felt like a living corpse, perhaps a zombie, after the Obliteration. His entire scientific life in the laboratory had been destroyed by the explosion. He wasn't even a fossil, because a fossil is a structure that lasts, and he would not last. No one does. Long before he had had to retract his Imagination gene, so that no longer existed either. He had sketched a face with tears in the margin of where he wrote that and drawn an arrow pointing to a few words about Thought-Particles, which said that was his major contribution.

He was happy, of course, that Rabbi Magnum, Rudy, picked up on the idea of Thought-Particles and made it a meaningful metaphor, but he wanted to make a scientific contribution. One contribution would be enough, he wrote. Very few scientists make a single new conceptual discovery. And then, sadly, he wrote how the Obliteration not only destroyed the Vision Science Center, but it also destroyed him. Everything he had worked on in his laboratory that had not been published yet—which included much of his research—was gone for good. Years of effort—poof—obliterated. He wrote about the fragility of life, as well as everything that seemed so important at one time—that it was no more lasting than a gust of wind. What good were imagination and effort? he wrote. It was all so transient. The diary broke Regina's heart.

She was surprised that there was no reference to Ricardo.

But then she arrived at the part she was hoping to find: his thoughts on the Obliteration. His exact words were crucial here, so she copied them down.

> *How could such a tragedy have occurred? Even more baffling, how was it possible that the cause had not been determined? Was it a conspiracy, or an act of a madman?*

So, Regina thought, he was asking the same questions that the journalist was asking now.

> *Maybe Alison was right, that it was a conspiracy. Her shady boyfriend, what's his name, the one who had weird friends, said it certainly was a conspiracy. He told me that he knew for sure it was a conspiracy!*

Oh, my god! Grandpa even underlined that the Obliteration might be a conspiracy.

> *The conspiracy is clear from the video of a truck with two people in it delivering desks. I was convinced when the sensitive microphone recorded something that sounded like "that should blast them off the planet." But the trouble is the exact words weren't clear when I played it back several times. Maybe it was something like "it would be a blast if we planted this video … I'm not sure what to make of it.*

Grandpa was telling the truth about having some information

that his dreams reflected what he had heard and possible causes—not the definite cause—for the Obliteration. And the video was a type of documentary film, at least in his fading memory. Who the heck was Alison? Grandpa had never mentioned her.

I don't know how much to trust Alison's friends anyway. One told me that he saw a strange group of pedestrians with matching tattoos on their necks that looked like igloos. It's nuts. I don't know. Maybe I'm mixing things up. Too bad they lost the video, so it all remains conjecture. I don't even know the name of Alison's friends, and she has disappeared. Too bad.

"I knew Grandpa wouldn't lie," Regina muttered to herself. "He would never lie, but he was imaginative. I'll give him that. He was just old, not senile. I've got to tell the world that. I will! But how?"

Chapter 16

REGINA WAS DETERMINED to rescue Grandpa and Ricardo from scientific obscurity. First, she had to truly believe that they should be rescued. It wouldn't work unless she was convinced and then hit on some truth. She thought of Ricardo in the mangrove swamp of Puerto Rico—what freedom she felt when that crossed her mind—discovering new phenomena of jellyfish and figuring out what they see, courageously speculating, with evidence—that was critical, having the evidence— that they see evolution, and then postulating that jellyfish have a brain. Hardly anyone, even scientists, knew that jellyfish have eyes. No one ever considered that they might have a type of brain. Wouldn't it be something if the brain was an outgrowth of an early eye, rather than eyes being outgrowths of the brain, as scientists thought? Scientists have barely scraped the surface of what's in front of them. Ricardo had given them new paths to understand the brain and evolution. These were important contributions then, and she believed they would become even more important in the future.

Grandpa's Thought-Particles never left Regina's mind. Did they exist? Did abstract thoughts have a counterpart in substance of some sort, as he predicted? Oh, my goodness, what an original question. What were Thought-Particles, and how did they work? Were these realistic questions that could be credited to Grandpa? Certainly. No question about that.

Many other thoughts kept her awake at night. Regina's mind was always in gear, never in neutral. How did something as complicated as people—as her—ever evolve? How did life itself come to be, or how was life even defined? She discarded the idea that God, or some supernatural force, created life. *Creativity*, not creation, *was* the world, at least that was her opinion. Creation was supernatural, religious, the work of a mysterious third party—a god. Creativity was different, it belonged to itself. Creativity was inherent, like a body part—a leg, or an arm, or a brain. Life wasn't created; it unfolded and evolved by the creativity of nature. Viruses and microorganisms and snails and baboons—everything alive—even thoughts—evolved because of the creativity of genes.

She had struggled with math and physics formulas at Princeton. Her instructor in physics thought that the universe could be explained by mathematics, but she didn't get it. How could math explain a rock or the sea or a leaf? At best, she thought, math could describe parameters, but not the origins of life. There was so much more that she wanted to understand. She had to go to a graduate school that would give her the background to answer at least some of her questions. The challenges were immense.

What did she need to know to exonerate Grandpa and Ricardo? How much was enough knowledge? The barrel of knowledge could never be filled. It was like time, which never ran out of space. She couldn't understand everything, and there was *so* much of everything. She had to accept that understanding just a few things might be okay.

What field of science should she apply to? While she had broad interests, she needed a specific target. Being interested in too many fields could be a burden. Grandpa often told her that one of her biggest problems was being able to succeed in too many areas. She used to take that as a compliment. Now she realized it had been a gentle way encourage her to be disciplined.

Perhaps thinking of a specialty was too detailed a question for now, before she knew the general area of her interests. She needed to discover a new universe that no one knew existed yet. *That* excited her. A new universe would be huge and complex with many parts. She thought big, and a universe was big, very much so. She could decide later which part of the new universe she would immerse herself in. Grandpa's and Ricardo's fields would fit somewhere within her new universe.

"That's essential," she told herself. "How else could I redeem them?"

A new universe! That was a trumpet announcing an adventure! But how to define or recognize a new universe? She would have to trust her gut, as Grandpa had told her.

She would apply to graduate schools and let fate do its job, like water flowing downhill. Physics had too much math, which was not for her, and chemistry was too analytical, so neither was a serious contender. Biology, her major in college, was her favorite subject. Physics and chemistry would provide a scaffolding for biology, but not the discipline itself. How long would it take her to discover a new universe? She had no idea.

What a challenge! Unreasonable? Perhaps. Was it "safe?" No. Was it "important?" Who knows? Safe and important were as hard to define as a universe. Regina thought that everything new was important. Queen Regina was searching for an imaginary castle in a new universe that hadn't been discovered yet.

How would she find her castle in that universe?

Chapter 17

Regina's first choice for graduate work was the California Institute of Technology—the famous Caltech—a relatively small and rigorous scientific institution. However, to be accepted as a graduate student was very competitive. She needed to write an essay about herself and her scientific interests. It excited her to combine her love of science with her love of writing, which continued to linger in the background. She would weave science into a narrative, partly true and partly fiction, as she did for her honor's thesis at Princeton—*A Lion's Universe, and I'm not Lying.*

"Bingo!" she muttered.

While she would apply to the department of biology—her passion—she still had to decide on the precise topic for her essay. The poorly defined idea of discovering a new universe, more a dream than anything else, was far too general and impossible to explain. The more she tried to conjure up some objective, clear subject in biology, the more her mind went blank. Then she wondered why she focused on being so innovative. No one is, or ever has been, completely original, not even Darwin or Freud or any iconic scientist. They were all influenced by their predecessors.

Perhaps she might consider artificial intelligence as an approach to biology. Biology and artificial intelligence overlapped, and Caltech excelled at both. There was no end to the advantages of having sophisticated robots that could learn and "think" in some way. Also, thinking was directly relevant to Thought-Particles. Thought and memory were among the most important yet least understood phenomena, and these phenomena overlapped with Ricardo's and Grandpa's work. She could also create robots that saw the future, a flipside of jellyfish seeing past evolution. But there already were many stories about robots and artificial intelligence, from reality to fantasy, and even horror. Robots were used as pets, service providers, information centers, armies, political rulers, even predators. She couldn't read everything that was already known or predicted about the subject, and she wasn't interested in rewriting the stories of others.

She let her imagination run wild and considered writing about constructing a type of black hole on earth. Perhaps the black hole could be used as a jail for prisoners sentenced to life without parole. Quite ridiculous, she thought, but fun! The prisoners could never escape or be released or pardoned because nothing gets out of a black hole, which raised questions about morality and forgiveness. Although those topics were not science, they were interesting. Were those at the forefront of *her* interests? Doubtful, yet she liked the mystery of black holes—their sheer power if nothing else. But she wasn't a physicist.

She wanted a subject at the heart of biology that was counterintuitive and ambiguous. Maybe a narrative about evolution. Ricardo's jellyfish seeing evolution and Grandpa's Thought-Particles were counterintuitive and certainly ambiguous. Even with the plethora of knowledge of genetics, the functions of most of the DNA in the genome of any species remained mysterious. That so much was known, yet so much remained unknown at the same time seemed an occupational paradox for any scientist. Perhaps exploring genes from new perspectives, not just DNA making RNA, would work. But how to look for encrypted phenomena without having a hypothesis of some kind, if only as a preliminary entrance point?

Another idea was the role of intermediates along the evolutionary pathway. Weren't Thought-Particles traveling from one person to another an intermediate for thinking and jellyfish seeing evolution a potential way to find missing intermediates? Such fantasy could include creating human successors, such as genetically engineered individuals able to live on other planets, foreshadowing the eventual need to escape extinction on a dying earth. As important as mutations and genetic engineering were, such a narrative seemed simultaneously too political and too fanciful and not original.

She felt depleted and became increasingly pessimistic as she wrote different drafts about over-inflated ideas. She was too tired to continue, so she put it aside and went to bed early.

Maybe it would appear clearer in the morning.

She wanted an original narrative for her application. What would that be?

Chapter 18

S HE SLEPT UNTIL ten the next morning and felt like a different person. But that wasn't the main benefit of her marathon sleep. It was her dreams, which had been vivid and relevant, as if they were real, not dreams at all. That wasn't just a trick of her imagination or forcing truth from where it didn't exist; the dreams *were* real, for her.

Not wanting to lose their meaning, she jotted down what she remembered of them, followed by her thoughts about the dreams. She called it an exercise in "dream reality."

Ricardo, thin, old, behind bars, was crying. Regina, in the background, heard him, which made her sad.

"Why are you crying?" she asked Ricardo.

"Because life is so short and I'm going to die without having done so many things I would have liked to do or should have done," he said. "I have failed."

"No one has done everything they want, and no one lives indefinitely," she answered, feeling that she was the failure, not Ricardo. But she wasn't in jail, Ricardo was, and she wasn't old enough to die. "Do you really believe you're a failure?" she asked him.

He didn't answer. A moment later he said, in her voice, "I judge my life by what I haven't done, what I've shied away from because it was too difficult or too frightening, not what I have done, which is never enough. Everyone is a failure."

Is that what I really believe? Regina asked herself, after she wrote down this part of her dream? How would I know what I didn't do, if I haven't done it? She felt she was going in circles but continued documenting her recollections anyway.

Another part of the dream started to invade her mind.

She saw Ricardo next to the cover of the novel Jellyfish Have Eyes. "I told you in my memoir about the trial for my squandering of government funds," Ricardo said, "about my life as a scientist."

Regina suddenly wondered, was Jellyfish Have Eyes a memoir? She thought it was a biography made into a novel with all sorts of made-up stuff. She had read the book twice. She was sure it was historical fiction, with Ricardo the protagonist, not the author.

"Of course it's a memoir," Ricardo insisted, interrupting her thoughts. "Do you think that someone else knew what I thought? As you've noticed, I wrote it under a pseudonym. Why did I do that if it was a memoir? Because it allowed me to say what I really thought."

The dream became blurry and slipped away from Regina's mind. She tried hard to reenter the dream, and slowly it crept back, but she wasn't sure if what she heard or saw or felt was really Ricardo or if she was now just trying to reconstruct the dream. The dream and her conscious reality were indistinguishable. Imagination and reality were the same in her mind.

"The moment anything comes out of my mouth—or out of anybody's mouth—naysayers come up with an endless array of criticisms. It gets tiring, and then I don't know who is right or what is the truth," Ricardo said.

Was that her thought as she was trying to recall the dream, or was it in the dream? She wasn't sure. As she was reflecting, she heard Ricardo's voice say, presumably in the dream,

"I was seeking questions, not answers. I didn't have a destination."

Again, she didn't know if that was in her dream or if she had made it up as she was writing. She didn't have a destination either, at least not yet. That hit a responsive note. Regina thought Ricardo's speculation that jellyfish have a brain of sorts and could visualize evolution was a brilliant leap to explore further, although his peers found it outlandish, impossible to prove then or probably ever, and dismissed the idea. It was too bold for the conservative scientists at the time. They limited their views to what fit best within existent knowledge and required preliminary evidence to support basic investigations. She believed that investigating the vast unknown by probing strictly what was known was somewhat of an oxymoron, even though it did make sense to ground basic research on a firm footing. Ricardo's speculations, based on his data, were science at its pinnacle. But why did she value Ricardo's research so highly if he discovered nothing that was accepted as fact? Was she taking on Ricardo's burden? Was her destination to be a pariah doomed for failure? Yes … perhaps …

Grandpa appeared in the dream next and said, "Stick to your gut instincts, Regina." Then he muttered under his breath, as he often did when alive, "Don't forget, all science, as factual as it is or strives to be, requires belief on your part and the acceptance of the world in which you live." His image disappeared, while his voice faded more slowly, leaving a short interval when she heard echoing, "Thought-Particles, Thought-Particles, Thought-Particles, I believe, believe, believe … "

Like Ricardo, Grandpa had the perspective of a life fully lived, not one in progress, as hers was. Both were now dead, yet what impressed Regina was that, even after death, they both realized in her dream that their life wasn't finished. No life was ever finished; no one had done everything they would have liked, or planned, to do. Everyone was a failure in that respect.

What, then, would Grandpa, buried in his coffin, tell her now?

Belief, she thought. Wasn't belief a requirement for fiction? Without belief, there's no story. Belief could never be proved, yet it drove life as well as fiction in many instances, religion being the most obvious example, but science too. Grandpa had written that in his memoir, *Roger's Thought-Particles*. She assumed now the apparent historical fiction was a memoir too.

Regina narrowed her eyes to slits, as she often did when she felt more confident in her thoughts. "Yes," she said to herself with determination, as she wrote that science was a human construct with traces of fiction in the form of speculation, and with enough belief to overcome the contradictions in its path.

She would write a short narrative—fiction—with science tiptoeing through it, with the themes of Ricardo's and Grandpa's unfinished lives. She would make up a story about a jellyfish that was able to think. How much fun it would be to let her fantasy romp amok in synchrony with her imagination and science! How would the admission department at Caltech react to her gamble? That was their decision, not hers. She began her short story …

Susan, the Lonely Jellyfish

Susan, the lonely jellyfish, evolved the first seeds of thought, the primordial evolution of the ability to think. Susan hadn't yet developed the ability to communicate her thoughts to other jellyfish, so they were trapped within her, like the active mind of a quadriplegic ALS patient. Not enough time had passed for the evolution of Thought-Particles. However, Susan's thoughts were her companion, making them a substance in function, if not in reality at the time. Since her thoughts couldn't be transmitted, they roamed in her mind as imagination.

Oh, how extraordinary the pathway of evolution!

Regina's hand shook when she clicked "send" for her application to Caltech. Her hope had switched to fear, worried that she had wrapped herself too tightly in the cloaks of Ricardo and Grandpa.

Chapter 19

S EEING CALTECH DISPLAYED on her ringing phone, Regina's heart
felt like it had kicked into a higher gear. It didn't settle down
on answering, as she was greeted with a formal sounding voice
saying, "I'd like to speak with Regina Resin, please."

"Speaking," she said calmly, belying her anxiety.

Why would they call? Admissions or rejections were always by mail,
electronic or otherwise. This was too soon for any decision. But …
what did they want …?

"I'm Dr. Jonathan Stark and I'm calling from Caltech's biology
graduate admissions department."

Regina didn't say anything, and Stark hesitated, leaving an uncomfortable gap of silence.

"We received your application and found it peculiar, to say the
least," he said.

That's for sure, Regina thought. But "peculiar" could mean strange-
weird or strange-interesting. Which was it?

"Peculiar? How so?" she said, trying to refrain from sounding
defensive.

"We were initially baffled and wondered whether you had mistakenly
sent the application to us instead of the humanities department. We
do have a humanities department at Caltech. Not everyone knows
that. A pretty good one too. And … hmmm … it might be easy to

make a mistake, I mean with Caltech being so science oriented and the pressure on you of sending applications all over the place. Did you mean to send your application to us or to the humanities department?"

A flame of anger lit up in Regina. Does he think that I'm not able to distinguish between the humanities and science?

"Nothing like that," she said emphatically, defensively, and then she caught herself and said politely, "I sent it to the biology admissions department. I'm applying to be a scientist."

"Really?" he still questioned.

It's hard to convince this guy that I'm not a moron, she thought, still angry, and then she reminded herself, once again, that an argument at this point wouldn't be the best idea.

"Yes, really. I didn't apply to any other graduate school. Stupid, I guess."

Why did I call myself stupid, she wondered? I shouldn't give him any ideas, or say that I feel dumb, which doesn't mean I *am* dumb. What's wrong with me? A story—fiction—for a science application? And only applying to one school? Why tell him that? And why was I stupid enough to do that? Just lazy?

"Well, yes. A first for us," Stark said. "We've never had an applicant send us a short story for a science admission. Well, that's not quite true. About eight or nine years ago, an applicant sent us a pretty good poem about science to let us know that he thought truth was beauty, and he wanted to devote his life to beauty."

"Did you accept him?"

"Of course not."

"Oh. So you're rejecting me," she said, as if it were a fact, not defensive any longer. "Why are you calling me instead of writing?"

The ball game was over, and she had lost. What would she do now? Start looking for other graduate schools, she guessed.

"We were intrigued when we noted you graduated *cum laude* from Princeton," he said. "That's an accomplishment. Princeton is not going to play tricks. It's a serious academic institution."

"Yeah. Thanks. That's right. No tricks," she said, flatly.

"Don't thank me yet," he said.

Did I thank him, she wondered? Why would I do that?

"My associates wanted to reject the application," he said. "Nothing against you personally. It's just that … we're hardcore science."

"I know," Regina muttered, wondering why he was going on and on about Caltech when he was rejecting her.

"You're original, I'll say that. And we looked up your honors thesis, which is on file in Princeton. It was pretty good. Maybe you should be a writer."

"I want to be a scientist." She wasn't negotiating.

"The story you sent us was short, but good. I liked it a lot. 'Susan, the Lonely Jellyfish' as the first steps for evolution of thinking and imagination. I think it's even better than your college story. Is it a habit of yours to write fiction to express science?" He didn't wait for the answer. "Anyway, the story is interesting. How did you ever dream it up?"

"I put some thoughts together. I took a chance and hoped that it wouldn't backfire at some point."

Why do I continue to be negative about everything? Her narrative science was becoming a trademark, and she liked it that way.

"I understand," Stark said. "Would you come for an interview next week?"

Is he serious? Would I come for an interview because I'm so strange?

"Do you mean that I might still be accepted?" she asked, incredulously.

"Don't jump the gun, Regina. We reject some amazing applicants. Believe it or not, we rejected the Nobelist James Watson of DNA fame way back in the twentieth century, and an array of other applicants who ended up with accomplished careers. It's always guesswork for us, who will succeed in the long run, and who won't. We're a small school and must be very selective."

Regina, stunned, was wildly excited. So, they're guessing that I might not be so dumb, she thought. Next week at Caltech for an interview! I might be accepted after all. Maybe my narrative science idea wasn't that foolish. Maybe … maybe …

THE FIRST THING she did when she hung up was make reservations to go to Caltech in Pasadena. After that, she wanted to tell Grandpa about it. If only he were alive. He wasn't, but she told him anyway in her mind. He was so happy that he shed a few tears for her, but then, typical of him, he warned her not to get too excited. She might not be accepted. She had to play it cautiously in the interview, not go overboard in explaining her interest.

I'll tell Mom and Dad tonight when Dad's home from work. Anyway, I'm not in Caltech yet. I may never be. But ... who knows?

To clear her mind and absorb this good news, even though she reminded herself several times that she hadn't been accepted yet, she went for a walk.

It was a good day, even though it was cloudy.

—⁂—

"MOM, DAD, I have exciting news!" Regina said at dinner that evening. She was beside herself with enthusiasm and hope.

"Oh. What about?" said Dad, as he slurped his soup.

"Caltech called," she said.

"Really?" Mom asked. "Don't they usually write responses, dear?"

Dad didn't say a word as he took another slice of bread.

"What did they say?" he asked finally.

"They want me to come for an interview next week. Isn't that great?"

"So, you're in? No more lounging around the house?" Dad asked, showing a bit more interest, but little tact or paternal enthusiasm.

"No. But I might be."

"Might be what ... in Caltech ... or lounging around the house?"

"Both. Either one or the other."

No wonder I'm so defensive, she thought.

Dad buttered his bread and sprinkled it with salt. "Well, have you got other choices if you're rejected?"

Regina remained silent. He didn't even know how many graduate schools she had applied to. She sure as hell wasn't going to answer him.

"Good luck, dear. Not everybody can be accepted you know," said Mom.

Regina didn't say another word throughout the dinner, and her parents didn't bring up Caltech again.

Dad was quieter than usual. Mom loved the chocolate cake dessert, and Dad watched TV after dinner.

Regina went to her room and felt like weeping. She didn't know if they were happy tears or sad tears. Both, she thought. It didn't matter. She was going to Caltech for an interview next week.

She had a new dream that night about "Regina, the Lonely Girl."

Chapter 20

REGINA ARRIVED FIVE minutes early for her interview at Caltech. The receptionist told her to be seated, and that Dr. Fuller would be there in a moment.

"Regina, glad to meet you," said Dr. Fuller when she appeared. She was at least six-foot tall and looked intimidating. "Please come into my office."

Regina took a seat in front of Dr. Fuller's desk. She felt especially small, smaller than usual, and worried that she was overdressed in a navy suit with her lucky gold ladybug—a high school graduation gift from Grandpa—pinned just above her heart. She was feeling clumsy walking in blue velvet shoes with 2-inch heels. She was accustomed to wearing running shoes, although she didn't like to run. She didn't know how Caltech types dressed. Dr. Fuller was in loose, bulky pants, a long-sleeved blouse, and sneakers. She looked stern, but her voice was soft, and that broke the tension a bit.

"Tell me about yourself, Regina. We haven't evaluated candidates using fiction as an application essay before, as Jonathan told you. He said you were determined to become a scientist—good for you—and advised us to interview you. I hope you weren't put off by his style. Many people find him abrupt, but he's actually a pussycat."

I guess being blunt has its benefits, especially to pussycats, she thought. She remembered that Grandpa had told her he was rewarded each time he was rude or plain angry at someone. He never understood why but said it seemed to be a sure way to get whatever he wanted.

"Clever idea, a fictional narrative to express science," Dr. Fuller continued. "Original. What a story! Ingenious, I would say. A lonely jellyfish who started the evolution of thinking and imagination. I especially liked the connection between thinking and imagination. So innovative. Anyway, why did you choose us for your graduate work, and what are your goals?"

Although Regina had prepared for these questions, she began to panic. She cleared her throat to stall and fidgeted in her seat.

Dr. Fuller smiled as if she understood. "I felt the same way when I interviewed for graduate school in Michigan twenty years ago," she said. "I feared being rejected, and I wasn't sure what my long-term goals were. I thought I wanted to be a researcher and told them I wanted to get a Ph.D. in inorganic chemistry. But when I had that degree and started doing research in the industry, I didn't like it. It was too removed from people. How much of a life would I have submerged in a pool of ions and catalysts? I realized I was a 'people person,' not a dispassionate scientist, although I did love science and admired scientists, at least the humble ones! It's a long story and you're being interviewed, not me, and here I am at Caltech admissions, talking about me rather than you. Sorry."

With every word that Dr. Fuller said, Regina's fear dropped a notch. She wanted to get up and hug her. Oh, my goodness. She wished Mom could have heard her, so supportive, so understanding. But she was happy that Mom wasn't there, that she was stuck at home with Dad and probably grocery shopping for dinner.

Why did she choose Caltech? That was Dr. Fuller's first question.

"I've applied to Caltech because, well, it's the best in science and as well as biology I'll get a thorough education in physics and chemistry and math, which I would never take the trouble to learn if they weren't required. I'm not very good at those subjects. Sounds ridiculous, no? Why apply to the Mecca of what I'm scared of? Because I know I'll need it for biology, which I've chosen because that's what I love. Biology is more conceptual, at least I think so, than the physical sciences, although I'll benefit greatly from more knowledge in the physical sciences. We know a lot about genes, metabolism, ecology, but still, they're not like physics or chemistry. Biology is ... conceptual, do you agree? Do you know what I mean? It requires more thinking than calculations. I like concepts more than numbers."

There, she thought. She'd given a plug to Caltech and not faked anything.

Dr. Fuller looked straight into Regina's eyes without flinching.

"That's the most honest answer I've ever heard," she said, after a short pause.

Regina wondered whether she was saying too much, too little, or something silly? Without realizing it, she was Grandpa's twin in some respects, fluctuating between overconfidence and insecurity, depending on how the stars were aligned. She continued.

"You want to know my goals as a biologist? I'm interested in thinking. I mean, in what's a thought? How does thinking work in the brain? Can a person transmit a thought at a different level than talking or making sounds, like I presume animals do?"

She realized she was taking on Grandpa's life, but it was sincere. She didn't mention Thought-Particles, at least not yet. She was applying, not Grandpa. Also, she had no bias toward Thought-Particles or any pre-conceived notion. Hadn't he said, like Ricardo, in so many words in her dreams, that although he was dead, his life wasn't finished? What did that mean anyway? She thought it meant that the important problems he had raised weren't answered yet.

"I'm not giving animals enough credit," she continued. "Animals don't just make random sounds. They have their own languages. How did thinking evolve? I bet so-called 'lower' animals, maybe even invertebrates like jellyfish—like Susan, the lonely jellyfish—aren't the only animals that think and imagine. That idea is fantasy today, I know. It seems impossible to study, like it was for defining genes or finding black holes some centuries back, until technology allowed genes and black holes to be studied, and what a thrill that must have been."

Grandpa's image appeared in Regina's mind, warning her to slow down, but she was on a roll. She knew that she shouldn't blabber and sprout stupid remarks. But Dr. Fuller seemed so kind; Regina felt that she could be herself. If they didn't want to accept her, so be it. There's nothing she could do about that. But she was independent, going solo, by herself, not attached to anyone. It was time she understood and accepted that. She had agency. Grandpa was dead, and her parents … well, they were in their own world.

"That's about it, Dr. Fuller. Who knows? I may end up doing something else with my degree, like you did, although I doubt it."

"You could become a writer, Regina. It's clear that you like that, and you certainly have the imagination and talent for it. Would that be bad?"

Would that be bad, Regina asked herself?

"I don't know what's good or bad, Dr. Fuller. Once I'm there, wherever 'there' is, I'll let you know. I do know, however, I will try my best at Caltech—if I get the chance, that is."

Regina was pleased with her answer.

They talked about politics and what kind of research was going on at Caltech and even about art. After fifteen or twenty minutes of bantering about this and that, Dr. Fuller said, "I've asked Phil Bradley, a second-year graduate student in biology, if he could show you around, and he said he would be happy to do that. I think you'll like him. He's very friendly. I'll buzz him in the lab. He'll be here in a few minutes."

—⁂—

PHIL KNOCKED ON Dr. Fuller's office door and entered.

"Hi," Regina said, in a friendly manner, attempting to camouflage the impact of seeing this tall, gorgeous man, with sandy hair overlying the tops of his ears, a goatee accentuating his slim face, and lovely gray eyes. And his smile. I've never seen a smile more inviting, she thought. His posture was erect and physically fit. She wondered if he regularly went to the gym or played some rigorous sport. It couldn't be skiing in sunny Southern California. Maybe hiking. She couldn't discern an ounce of superfluous fat covered by his T-shirt. He's … just amazing, she thought. She even let her imagination drift, imagining what a perfect match for her slim, yet strong, healthy body he would be. Suddenly, he was more interesting than science, and at Caltech, that was something! How unexpected, having believed that Caltech was filled with nerds glued to the laboratory bench or computer.

"You would be happy here," he said, as they strolled to his lab so that he could show her what he was working on.

"Are you happy with Caltech, with your mentor, your peers, you know, the general atmosphere here?"

"Absolutely, but it's a lot of work. Every graduate student needs to have taken all the courses that an undergraduate would have had in their field. I'm a biologist, but I needed to take courses in quantum mechanics, thermodynamics, statistical mechanics, and the list goes on. It's an eye-opener, but I've really learned a lot."

Fear suddenly overwhelmed Regina. Would she be able to pass all those requirements? He put her to rest.

"Don't worry, Regina. It's not that hard, and there's always someone around who is happy to help you if you need it. Another graduate student helped get me through thermodynamics, which I hated. Everyone needs some guidance from time to time. Anyway, I almost never work on weekends. That's when I run. Someday I hope to run the Boston marathon. I'm from Boston."

That explains the perfect body, she told herself. The only thing she liked about running was the shoes.

He doesn't work on weekends? Isn't he ambitious or anxious to do his experiments, she wondered? I couldn't stay away from my research every weekend. I'd be curious to find out what my experimental results were or, if I hadn't done any experiments, I'd want to get started doing some, not wait until Monday. Her mind was wandering as if she was already a graduate student there and she again had to remind herself that she hadn't been accepted yet.

"Here's my lab. The tanks hold various crustaceans," Phil said while casually waving his hand in their direction. "I'm the only marine biologist here. Most everyone is doing molecular genetics or computer-related studies on some technical problem. The lab next to mine is comparing the genes expressed in brains of different species, or something like that."

Regina lit up. "That sounds fantastic," she said. "What professor is doing that?" She wondered how she could map genes responsible for thinking and imagination in any species.

"Dr. Andrew Slingsby. He's very ambitious. Yeah, it's interesting, but I'd never want to do that. It's complicated and those guys work all the time."

"Weekends too, I bet," she added, with a light touch.

"Yup. Day and night. That's out for me."

Mr. Sexy just slipped a notch or two in her book, while science rose to the top again.

"Here's what I'm doing. Did you know lobsters have noses? Well, they do. Not many people know that. I'm trying to figure out how smell affects their behavior. Weird, eh?"

"How do you think smell works for lobsters?"

"Probably guides them to food or repels them from danger in some way."

That seems limited, she thought. "Do you know the different substances they can detect by smell? Do you think their noses have a social or sexual function for them? Perhaps they recognize kin by smell?" Her mind started working overtime. She even thought of a possible short story about a lobster community ruled by smell. Hmmm ...

"Maybe," he answered, but she didn't know which question he was answering. "I hope to have my degree in two more years, but it may take a little longer. I'll show you around the campus. A lot of important work is done here, stuff that leads to Nobel Prizes."

The campus was well-groomed and packed with modern buildings that must have been buzzing with activity, like the Vision Science Center had been when Grandpa worked there. She imagined an empty field with a few dying California oak trees if Caltech suffered a similar Obliteration.

When they walked to the cafeteria for a cup of coffee, a gust of wind blew away the smog hiding the mountains, which stretched to the sky directly behind Caltech. The mountains were so close she could almost reach out and touch them.

"Where did *those* come from?" she asked Phil, pointing to the mountains.

"Oh, that damn smog! It's amazing how it conceals the mountains.

It's hard to breathe in it sometimes too. It really bothers me when I run. It hurts my lungs. Los Angeles has been smothered in smog forever. I guess nothing is perfect," he said.

That's right, Regina thought. Nothing is perfect. Not Grandpa dying, not her parents, not Phil, probably not even Caltech.

"It's not unlike our situation as people," she told him. "We're hidden to some extent by our own personal 'smog,' until the wind blows and there we are, as naked as the day we were born. And we're definitely not perfect."

Regina wondered where that little outburst had come from.

Phil smiled. "I guess."

Since her return flight wasn't until the next morning, Phil took her to a small party with a group of his friends in the evening. They were all extremely welcoming and she had a good time, though the loud music sounded more like noise to her.

"I love that band," Phil told her when it got even louder. He started dancing with himself. "It makes me want to run," he said.

Me too, she thought, but in the opposite direction.

Back in the hotel, she reflected on the interview. It had gone okay. And she liked Phil, despite his apparent shallowness. What a great-looking guy! And so friendly. He even got her interested in marine biology. But lobsters smelling to get food, music banging away on her eardrums, no work on weekends, running instead of doing experiments?

What's more, she realized Phil had never asked what her main interest was in science.

—⁂—

WHEN SHE FLEW home to Elizabethtown the next day, she worried that she had flubbed the interview. She thought she'd probably talked too much and didn't know whether trying to study the evolution of thinking made any sense. Exposing ideas and taking responsibility for them always gave her pause. It was different from keeping the ideas to herself. Dr. Fuller probably thinks I'm full of it, she thought. Evolution of thinking is a castle in the air, like imagination. At least it's *my* castle, she told herself. Well, not entirely. Ricardo and Grandpa had something to say about thinking first.

How to study what one doesn't understand, she wondered? One needs some type of foundation to build upon. At least she knew what she wanted to study—thinking and imagination—and she knew she wanted to redeem Ricardo and Grandpa's reputations. Her focus now was whether she would be accepted at Caltech and, if she was, how to begin to achieve those lofty goals.

When she went to bed that night, she remembered that Phil had an adorable wobble when he walked. But he liked to run, not walk. He wondered what lobsters smelled. She would have preferred to know what lobsters thought about.

Chapter 21

Two weeks later Regina received a special delivery letter from Caltech. They had told her that they don't use electronics to communicate regarding admissions, an eccentric holdover from days past that they maintained. She tore open the thin envelope and removed the single sheet containing only a few lines. Her heart sank, thinking a short letter meant lack of interest. But ...

Dear Ms. Resin,

Congratulations! We are pleased to inform you of your acceptance to Caltech's biology division as a Ph.D. candidate, starting on September 15, 2191. There will be five other candidates entering with you in the biology department. Please arrive by September 12, which is when orientation starts.

As customary for our graduate students, you will receive a full academic scholarship and a small stipend for being a teaching assistant—which graduate students are expected to do—running the undergraduate laboratory courses. Details to follow.

Sincerely yours,

Eleanor Fuller, Ph.D.

Graduate Admissions Department

California Institute of Technology

Underneath the signature was a handwritten note: "*A hearty congratulations, Regina! I'm so happy for you and wish you luck in your studies. I'm sure you will thrive here. Eleanor*"

Regina was beside herself. Was this true? Was someone playing a joke on her? Of course not. She reread the letter four times, and then she read Eleanor's note at least six times, slowly—it took her over a minute. This was for real. She sat down and closed her eyes, immersed in this magic moment. She was accepted as a Ph.D. student at Caltech, a miracle so rare that only a very few people have such good luck to experience it. Regina felt the full impact at her core for a minute or so, as she floated lightly in dreamland, by herself.

She wanted to call Phil and tell him, but she would see him soon enough. Maybe he knew already. No, doubtful.

"I'm happy for you, dear," Mom said when Regina told her. Then she looked at her watch. "Oh, it's later than I thought. I must go grocery shopping before the store closes. We're out of milk for breakfast. Let's talk later."

Regina had learned not to be disappointed by her mother's lukewarm reaction to her sizzling success. She understood. Mom had never undertaken such a difficult and uncertain challenge—had never put her life on the line, so to speak—so, of course, she couldn't feel what Regina did.

"I have to be there by September 12 for orientation, Mom."

"That's wonderful, dear," Mom replied. "We'll need to go shopping to make sure you have the right clothes for California."

Regina's Dad's reaction was different. "Oh. Good. Congratulations. A scholarship, and a stipend for being a teaching assistant. Wonderful."

That was it. He didn't have to cough up a pretty penny.

She was the luckiest girl in the world.

Chapter 22

Regina buried herself at Caltech, struggling at first with the obligatory courses that Phil had told her about in the physical sciences. They were less difficult than she had imagined, but she did need to work every weekend, when Phil was out running. She was happy that she could keep up with the courses. Phil asked her how she liked taking all those difficult subjects that weren't directly related to her research.

"It's fine," she said. "I'm gaining a science foundation that may be useful and could be important for me in the future. At least I know what they are all about, which will let me know if they might be useful."

Regina also knew that she wanted to prove to herself that she could handle the rigors of Caltech. Didn't everyone have something to prove?

"You've got a better attitude than I had," said Phil. "I don't see why anyone needs to know much about fields that are not directly relevant to their work. Does an astronomer need to be a paleontologist, or a physicist need to be an ecologist?"

"Maybe not, Phil. But you never know. Concepts of physics may be important to understand ecology, and as for an astronomer—they shoot for the stars anyway. They should know everything."

"Very funny!"

Regina and Phil became good friends. They often had brainstorming sessions together about their research as well as broader issues of life. Of course, her peers in the laboratory, who put science above any other interest, asked poorly disguised questions about whether she had any romantic intentions with him. She played coy, enjoying capturing their imagination, for imagination had always been her favorite topic that applied to everything.

"He's very nice," she might say. "I love being with him."

When she used the word "love," they perked up and probed to get more on the subject. Sometimes she might oblige them by saying, "We help each other interpret our
    experiments."

"That's all?" some might say.

"Oh no," she teased them. "We talk about our favorite foods and movies and stuff like that."

She never satisfied her friends' curiosity but enjoyed leading them on. That was a new experience in social relations for her. As for the honest answers to their questions? Well, she didn't know what they might be. Thus, she told them the truth. Nothing she said implied romance, but none of her answers explicitly excluded it.

HAVING COMPLETED CALTECH's course requirements, Regina plunged into research on gene expression in the fly brain. Andrew Slingsby, who had the laboratory adjacent to Phil's, was her mentor. He was brilliant, she thought, and informal, insisting from the beginning on being called Andrew. We're all equal, he said, just at different stages in our careers. He was a laissez-faire type, leaving her reasonably independent in directing her research. That was fine with her and gave her a valuable learning experience. The less she was told what to do, the happier she was. Volumes were already known about the fruit fly, *Drosophila*, since its genetics, development, behavior, and function had been investigated intensely for almost two centuries. There was more already known about *Drosophila* than she could ever find the time to read. Yet she was among the first to study the functional organization of the tiny fly brain. She had no illusion that she would discover whether flies think or imagine anything, but she hadn't forgotten her interest in that. She was aware that her research contributions would no doubt be lost in the hundreds—thousands—of research articles that had been published already on the fly. She made the analogy that her thesis research was like driving on a paved highway in a traffic jam. That was all right, since her goal as a Ph.D. student was to learn techniques that would help her develop new ways to study the evolution of thinking when she had her own laboratory. She hadn't forgotten her self-imposed challenge that somehow, someday, she wanted to exonerate Ricardo and Grandpa with her discoveries and elevate their legacies in the history of science.

She also hadn't forgotten her dream to discover a new universe after she graduated, whatever that really meant. The specific problems she had in mind for the future were: What exactly is a thought in terms of brain activity? How did the ability to think evolve? What happens in the brain when someone had a sudden thought, like an epiphany? These questions, rooted in neuroscience, were extreme challenges. She certainly wouldn't be able to skip work on weekends or get sidetracked with hobbies.

She often told herself how lucky she was when she was buried in her work, alone, and not sure where all the effort would take her, if anywhere. "Most people spend their life searching for something they can immerse themselves in. I have it. Lucky me!" was her standard answer when someone asked her if she was happy at Caltech.

—◊◊◊—

THE TIME PASSED quicker than she anticipated, and in a short four years she was ready to defend her thesis. Phil, although a year ahead of her, still needed another year before he could graduate. It turned out that lobster noses played more important behavioral roles than he had realized.

Regina was nervous but self-assured as she stood in front of five professors, each a world authority in their field, for her oral examination. She wore the same navy-blue suit with the lucky gold ladybug pin that

Grandpa had given her, and she wore her shoes with the 2-inch heels, as she had done for her interview with Eleanor. Never mind that she was overdressed. She wanted to repeat her past success in her interview for admission to Caltech. She would leave Caltech well-dressed and determined, if still somewhat insecure. Even the most hard-core rationalists are susceptible to superstition at some times in their life.

The exam went without incident. She kept her answers brief and precise, having learned that less was often more. Her fanciful ideas and speculations and dreams were her business. She wouldn't go on and on with her thoughts just to hear her own voice. One hour later felt like only a few minutes had passed. Suddenly, she was reborn from Regina Resin to Dr. Regina Resin—*doctor*! Finally.

Phil was the first to congratulate her. He was genuinely happy for her, and that meant a lot to her. He was probably the only one who had been truly in her camp since Grandpa died. Mom and Dad sounded happy for her on the phone. Of course. They were her parents. They now had a doctor in the family, even though she knew nothing about medicine.

It didn't take long to remind herself that her transformation was from a protected small fish as a Caltech graduate student, to an unprotected, more vulnerable small fish in the perilous sea of reality. Many small fish get eaten by big fish; a few, however, survive.

She planned to survive.

Interesting, she thought, prestige, as well as vulnerability, increased like electron energy levels—in quantum leaps—not in gradual increments as might seem intuitively the case. She wondered what the rules were governing the space between the energy levels, where she felt she was now.

Chapter 23

Regina didn't want to waste time with more training as a postdoctoral fellow in someone else's laboratory after receiving her Ph.D. She was anxious to be independent.

"One never knows enough," she told Andrew. "When should I set out on my own? I'll need to learn new techniques, trends, opinions forever—progress never ends—which, ironically, may not always be progress. I might as well begin learning how to stay up to date."

"So, what's your plan, Regina?" he asked, without voicing his opinion.

"I want a research position in a marine laboratory so I can investigate the octopus's brain," she said.

Andrew raised his eyebrows. He had expected her to continue her research on the fly. She had identified a new gene expressed highly in the fly brain, and its function remained unknown.

"Octopus brains? From flies to octopus? Why? Because octopus are bigger?"

"Maybe," she said. "But the star-sucker pygmy octopus is smaller than an inch. Okay, I admit it. That's bigger than a fly."

She summarized her thinking for him. There have been numerous attempts to evaluate intelligence in vertebrates, she said, especially mammals, concentrating on primates. Large-brained whales and dolphins have complex behaviors with their own language and cognitive skills. Not too much is known beyond that, at least to my knowledge. Wouldn't it be great to have a way to know whether they think or imagine anything, and if so, how it might be similar or different from humans? Birds, too, show signs of a rich cognitive existence. These are all vertebrates.

"It's a different story for invertebrates," she said. "Are they intelligent, and do they have an inner cognitive life? There's increasing interest in the subject, but no one speaks their language, assuming they have one. No one takes invertebrates very seriously in that regard. No one lives in the same culture as non-human vertebrates, much less invertebrates. "Ignorance rules the day. The possibility of invertebrate intelligence seems far-fetched. I doubt anyone would say a snail is intelligent."

Andrew nodded in agreement, while Regina was thinking about Ricardo's forgotten studies on jellyfish. Jellyfish were at the very beginning of animal evolution, and Ricardo had suggested that jellyfish already had a simple brain of some sort, even if it was diffuse rather than concentrated as a specific organ.

"Octopus are an exception," she said. "They seem to be much smarter than other invertebrates."

"I know, although I haven't thought much about those animals."

Regina said that she thought that invertebrates, including flies, were ripe for investigating whether they think and learn. Humans couldn't be the only species that think, she said repeatedly. The ability to think must have evolved.

"Honestly, even if not groundbreaking yet, or perhaps never, don't you think it might be adventuresome to study the differences in expressed genes between the brains of trained and wild-type octopus? To me, research means never quite being sure what I'm doing, because research requires us to learn *everything* we can. If we knew the answers, it wouldn't be research. Right? I'm still looking for the right question. I know. It's a big chunk to chew."

Regina was thinking that neither Ricardo nor Grandpa knew exactly what they were doing. Maybe she could help them in retrospect. But she did worry that she might get lost like they did.

"You're very ambitious, Regina, and I respect that. But I worry that you might be taking on a morass of unclear questions. Gamblers seldom win. Finding a new gene highly expressed in the fly brain is very good work, congratulations on that. Your publication was well received, and you could create a blueprint of how to study it further. Since so much is known about *Drosophila*, it's likely that whatever your results, they would fit within a pattern of previous work by a lot of researchers in the field. Your gene may even link its expression with abstract brain processes—who knows—which is what you always talked about."

She too was worried and knew his caution was on the mark. The fly gene she had discovered that was expressed highly in the fly brain was interesting and needed characterization. She could learn a lot about it by applying available techniques that were used by many scientists. Following that path would be the safest research route to take and would undoubtedly advance science. She might even discover that it was related to flies thinking, but that was a long shot if there ever was one. Yet, once again, she thought of Ricardo and Grandpa, not in detailed scientific terms or with regard to what experiments she thought about doing, but about extending their careers, bringing them back to join her in research, in her mind. She thought it doubtful that following up on her fly work would blend well with their work.

With a strong recommendation from Andrew and two other professors at Caltech, she was offered the opportunity to work independently at the Friday Harbor Laboratories, a branch of the University of Washington on San Juan Island in Puget Sound, with the condition that she obtain a research grant for support. Not only was it a beautiful place, away from distractions, but the basic research at the Friday Harbor Labs was along the lines she wanted to take. The famous green fluorescent protein, invaluable for basic and medical research to investigate gene expression of jellyfish, was discovered there long ago, which led to Osamu Shimomura, Martin Chalfie and Roger Tsien receiving the 2008 Nobel Prize in Chemistry.

Discovering nature's secrets by exploring little-studied species was a perfect fit for Regina and in the spirit of Ricardo's jellyfish research.

She started her research in Puget Sound while she applied for a government grant and learned how to capture octopuses. She trained a few to choose between differently shaped signals to receive food, impressing her colleagues at the laboratories with her dedication to research.

Regina did have one distraction: Phil. He had finished his graduate work and unexpectedly appeared at the Friday Harbor Labs to continue his research on lobster noses. They became ... well, friendlier than before ... and spent time conversing, hiking, rowing in the Sound, and watching movies on the computer now and then, although mostly they worked on their separate projects. He was always willing to take time off to explore the islands in Puget Sound or go running. Regina enjoyed his company but was reluctant to be diverted from her research. When they were together, she always insisted on getting back to her lab to do more work before the day ended, even when he tried his best to convince her that there was more to life than her research.

Chapter 24

On A crisp sunny spring day in the early morning, Regina went to the cafeteria and sat at a table in the corner so that she wouldn't be bothered. She wanted to review her progress and plan new experiments.

"Hi there, Regina," Phil greeted her, holding two cups of coffee, one for him and one for her. He sat down next to her as if she had nothing better to do than talk to him. "What's up?" he said.

She was frustrated to be interrupted.

Phil ignored her annoyed tone when she answered. Rather, he smiled from ear to ear, his trademark greeting.

"Oops, sorry, your majesty. Are you preparing to party with your friendly octopuses?"

She forced a smile. She wished she didn't have dark circles under her eyes, which she'd noted when she got dressed in the morning. Maybe she looked better now. She was wearing her favorite bright orange sweater that fit snugly, almost revealing. Phil could be annoying, but he looked handsome in his Dartmouth sweatshirt, with stains that showed its history. He wore it casually, like it was part of his body.

"The collecting boat is going out in an hour to get some giant shrimps," he said. "I'm going for the ride. Want to come along? They might catch an octopus for you by chance. The boat captain told me that they nabbed one the other day. It's amazing how often they find a new species of some kind. Maybe they will find something new today. Anyway, it'll be relaxing. The sun hasn't shone so brightly, and the sea hasn't been so blue in a long time. Want to come along?"

At that moment, light flashed through the window, as a few small clouds crossed the path of sunlight. It felt as if the outside had entered the cafeteria and found its way to her, trying to tell her something … but what? Probably to go for the ride since the sunshine and calm weather were exceptional and wouldn't last forever. Nothing does.

"Sounds fun, Phil."

—⁂—

THE WATER WAS like a lake on a windless day: not even ripples on the surface. Regina needed sunglasses to shield her eyes from the bright light reflecting on the water. Mt. Baker's snow-covered peak rose majestically in the distance.

The boat skimmed along, pushing aside jellyfish near the surface of the water and causing a pleasant stream of warm air to brush Regina's face. Her mind moved along from thought to thought as well. Did jellyfish really have brains and see evolution, as Ricardo thought? A humpback whale flipped its mammoth tail—fluke—in the air as it dived into the depth far from the boat. She had read that female whales did this to attract males. Whales lived in their hidden world of language and behavior with so many unknowns. What do they think about with their big brains? When do different lifestyles create different universes of existence? All animals breathe the same oxygen, whether in the air or dissolved in the water, on the same planet. What's a universe? What differentiates one universe from another?

"Regina … Regina … World to Regina." She heard Phil's voice getting louder with each word.

"Oh, sorry. My mind drifted and I was daydreaming. It's so different … totally different from our world."

"What's different?"

"The sea world."

"You're right. But while you were in dreamland, guess what the dredge brought up? A crazy new fish species with an extra set of gills on each side. It's amazing!"

Regina went to see the weird fish. How was it possible to see new species so often when dredging in the same place for so many years? How many species existed in the mysterious aquatic environment? How many had never been seen before? Only humans took a census every ten years, and even those weren't that accurate.

"How do you know this is a new species without examining its genes, Phil? Maybe it's a mutant of some type?"

Phil thought about that for a moment and said, "Good point. But aren't different, closely related species just adapted mutants?"

Yes, they were, she thought.

—⁓—

Suddenly, Regina felt that she was an amalgamation of herself and Ricardo and Grandpa, yet she also felt distinct from them. How strange, she thought, to be an individual and others at the same time. She remembered Ricardo's dream as he described it in his memoir. Jellyfish *"pulsed in synchrony as if linked, yet each was an individual, alone, like him ... They dissolved and reformed, over and over again, dissolving and reforming, merging and separating."* Yes, she felt like a jellyfish in Ricardo's dream.

A moment later, she remembered Grandpa telling her that he believed the transfer of Thought-Particles blended minds and ideas between individuals, so everyone was also a part of everyone else. Had she joined her deceased scientific kin while she was still alive? Had she inherited their demons as well?

Her head felt as free as a helium balloon floating in the sky, and as buoyant as a puffer fish drifting in the sea until it deflated to its proper size. But she was neither Ricardo, the Argentinean intellectual warrior, nor Grandpa, the intellectual and accidental success. She was the same person she always was, Queen Regina—royalty in her private kingdom—still alive with a future.

She closed her eyes and bathed in the soothing sensations of the rhythmic rocking of the boat and the warmth of the sun and the gentle breeze, and imagined the environment receding until it disappeared, leaving her suspended in a black and noiseless void. Was she in the new universe she sought? The universe seemed both familiar and foreign, as if she had always inhabited it and yet joined it now for the first time. Her universe didn't foresee a future or explain the past. It formed no image in her mind, as did the vast reality universe of endless spacetime, supposedly curved, with stars and black holes and dust and cosmic radiation and meteors. She hadn't discovered a new galaxy or a new life form at the bottom of the ocean. Regina's new universe was in her mind.

She wondered if a comparable internal universe also existed in Phil's mind, or anyone else's mind. If so, was it the same, or different for everyone? Did it feel different for each person, as do personal experiences? Her new universe included imagination but seemed more than an ability to have abstract thoughts and see images and feel senses in her mind. Her new universe was greater than imagination by itself: it was an entire *imagination universe*.

"Perhaps," she said softly, "the imagination universe contains what I imagine even before I imagine it."

The new universe was mysterious in its complexity. She wondered how her mind could contain such a huge universe that was separate from the reality universe she also inhabited. She assumed that humans and, she believed, all animals inhabited the new universe in some fashion. There was no need to explain imagination to anyone because everyone knew what it was, or thought they knew what imagination was. Ricardo and Grandpa had it in abundance. But did they realize that they inhabited an entire imagination universe? Did anyone realize that their imaginations were only a small part of the imagination universe?

Regina asked herself, what about proof? Can a concept found in the imagination universe be proved in the reality universe? Possibly, she thought. Was an epiphany, as Ricardo had for jellyfish seeing evolution, and that Grandpa had for proximity being essential for the transfer of Thought-Particles, a proof? Could anything be proved if it resided in the imagination universe?

These thoughts were so ephemeral. She was getting tangled up and confused by all the strands of thought flopping around. Never mind about proof now. That's a secondary occurrence in the reality universe. Creativity flowers and science soars in my imagination universe, she thought. It's so quietly beautiful, without noise or rules. It's both science and art.

"Regina, are you okay? You look pale. You're not seasick on this flat sea, are you?" Phil asked.

She didn't react immediately, as if she was having difficulty waking up from some deep space.

"Regina! Do you hear me?"

"Oh, sorry. Yes. I hear you. Sorry. I'm fine, Phil. I just had a few thoughts," she said, in a very low voice. "Just some thoughts. Or were they dreams?"

Chapter 25

WHEN REGINA RETURNED from the boat ride, she was curious to check out what neuroscientists thought about imagination, beyond the obvious that it's a process in the brain. But how did the brain create imagination? She surfed online and learned that imagination stimulates electrical activity in the free-associative regions of the human brain, which includes most of the surface of the cerebral cortex and receives input from numerous other regions of the brain as well. Thus, much of the brain contributes to imagination, unlike the well-known senses that are delimited mostly to specific areas in the brain. Imagination isn't confined! It's huge and uses the whole brain! It's like a mental universe!

It would be great, she thought, if she could compare brain activities between humans and octopuses, or any other animals, while they're imagining. But how would she know whether an animal was imagining? Maybe it would work the other way around: certain brain activity might tell her when the animal was imagining. All this was guesswork, of course, awaiting more knowledge.

"This is becoming impossible," she muttered, frustrated, and recalling the warning she received from Andrew that she might be undertaking too much of a risky, poorly defined research project. She felt lost. How to even know when an important question is too complex to try to answer? "It's like I'm looking at a small pile of bricks to use for constructing a sixty-story building and not even knowing what kind of building I want to build," she said to no one in particular.

Wait, she thought. Am I not a basic scientist because I'm drawn to things I don't understand? Why is that? She paused until the answer came to her. It's because when the image is clear and the puzzle is solved, when there's general agreement about the cause and mechanism of the phenomenon, there's little use for imagination, except, perhaps, looking for a practical application.

She had no idea where her curiosity was going to take her. It's the hope and personal involvement and mystery, she thought. That's what drives me.

Phil suddenly appeared and looked as if he was in the doldrums.

"My favorite lobster died, the one I was using for most of my experiments. I can't win. Who cares about lobster noses anyway? I should quit science."

"Cheer up. It can't be that bad," she said. This wasn't the first time he'd talked about quitting science. Quitting wasn't a realistic topic for her.

"What would you do if you did quit?"

He sighed. "I don't know. Maybe become a physical education teacher in high school or something like that."

After a moment, he showed her a bag filled with live shrimp. "I salvaged these from our boat trip. How about cooking them in seawater over a Bunsen burner in the lab for an early dinner? I'm sick of cafeteria food and I'm not in the mood to do any experiments tonight."

She was hungry too, although she could have continued talking about science all night. But that wasn't Phil's idea of fun.

He heated the water, which boiled in a few minutes.

"Are you going to throw those innocent shrimps into that torture chamber?" she said, her face in a grimace.

"I don't plan to eat them live," he said, and dumped all the shrimps into the boiling water.

Regina was horrified when she looked at the squirming, dying shrimps. "They must be in terrible pain, Phil. Do you think they're aware of what's going on?" She fought her empathy and looked away from them.

"They're shrimp, Regina, dumb, thoughtless, edible shrimp, and I'm hungry. Delicious too, I might add."

Regina didn't buy that. "It's so cruel," she said. "First these harmless, innocent creatures not doing any harm are captured as if they were prisoners of war, when there's no war, and then boiled to death. It's ... I don't know ... it's not right."

She remembered reading that Ricardo had had the same thoughts when he collected jellyfish for his research. She felt a stone fall into her stomach and lost her appetite. She would eat a few, but how could Phil not understand? Even when his favorite lobster died, he only cared that his experiment was ruined. She felt overcome by the cruelty and indifference of the world, and the journalist suddenly appeared in her mind. Phil didn't look quite the same.

He fell quiet, looking disappointed that his plan for a romantic dinner was going down the drain.

"Do you know that mantis shrimp have twelve different opsins which potentially makes them able to see more colors than any known creature on earth? That's why they're called peacock mantis shrimp. Also, they can wallop a punch with their claws and have even been noted to break the glass of an aquarium. Do you really want to eat that for dinner?"

Phil looked dumbfounded. "Really? But these aren't mantis shrimp, are they? And I'm hungry."

"Sometimes the world sucks," she added, looking disturbed and sad. "It doesn't matter who you are or where you are. You could be a king in your palace or a prisoner in jail and have lots of reasons, personal ones of all types, to be angry and frustrated and just plain paranoid."

She had targeted the journalist in her mind, although she didn't mention her. How she hated that woman! She also thought of Ricardo, who had rotted in jail as a felon for having had imaginative insights, and Grandpa, whose Thought-Particle theory was ignored by scientists. All that was cruel and unfair.

"Wow! A king in my palace. That sounds interesting," Phil said, scratching his head. "I don't know about being in jail, I'm no felon, and I'm not royalty, that's for sure. Seems I'm only a shrimp executioner"

Regina didn't respond. She did, however, wonder if anything ever bothered him. Did he have any reasons to complain like she did? He always seemed pleased, never tormented. It was annoying. Was he really free of vulnerabilities, or was he just hiding them?

"I'm not making fun of you, or angry. Honest," Phil said sheepishly, looking self-conscious. "Did I say something wrong?"

"No," she said. "You're always honest."

She liked him, but … well, liking wasn't loving.

A sudden thought invaded Regina's mind. Could she create an imaginary world that could displace the real world? Could she make an imaginary Utopia exist as a reality? She recalled the blur she had experienced when she had discussed the role of imagination for a writer or scientist with Grandpa. Now similar thoughts and questions were clearer, more focused. Where was the dividing line between reality and imagination that danced in the lush green valley of hope, as well as in the burning pits of hell?

"Phil, what do you think of imagination? Could it be real as well as abstract?"

"What do you mean, *real*?"

"Could imagined things exist? You know, like a cartoon is real for a kid? Would it be possible for you to imagine a tree or a house until it becomes real, at least for you? Or is your imagination always trapped in your head, a never-come-true abstraction? Is imagination a topic for science, especially if what's imagined can't be proved, or at least hasn't been proved yet?"

She was entering dangerous territory. Was she joining Grandpa in his hopeless trap of proving the existence of Thought-Particles, which no one could identify? Was she heading for disaster, as her mentor had warned her?

"Are you kidding, Regina? Imagination is something that exists in the brain. Of course, it's important for science. It's important for anything creative or remembered or just about everything. I don't get what you mean."

Regina was struggling to understand exactly what she was after.

"I wonder, if imagination can't be proved and remains an abstraction in one's brain, is it only fantasy? If so, and if it can't ever be physically grasped, does it exist? Am I making sense? Don't answer that. I'm not sure what I mean myself. For imagination to be science, it would need proof. Right?"

Phil rolled his eyes. "You're going off the deep end, Regina."

He just didn't get it. Such a nice guy, a perfect match, but for whom?

"Hmmm ... Regina, this is getting too complicated for me, but it does make me think about things. When I think of imagination, I think of dreams. We all have them. They're abstractions that don't need proof to be considered real. They exist, right? Could anyone say that dreams don't exist because they haven't been proved? Yet they're a product of our imagination. Would you agree that dreams are abstract happenings that are real but can't be proved? I've always been worried about dreams. They're my Achilles' heel."

Regina sat up straight as a board. Phil *does* have a vulnerability, an Achilles' heel. Dreams!

"Why?" she asked. "Why were you, or are you, worried about dreams?"

"It's a long story, but ... well, my dreams aren't always fantasy. Sometimes they're reality."

"What do you mean? I'm curious."

She wasn't talking only to Phil anymore. Grandpa had just joined the conversation in her mind; never mind that he wasn't there. Dreams were a big deal to everyone, no matter who they were. Everyone dreamed.

"How would you feel if you were dreaming that you were eating a cheese sandwich, woke up, and found yourself doing exactly that: eating a cheese sandwich?" Phil asked. "A cheese sandwich isn't that terrible. What if you dreamed that you were stabbing your dog and woke up and saw your pet bleeding to death, and a bloody knife in your hands."

"Did that happen to you?" Regina asked, alarmed.

"No. Nothing like that. But the cheese sandwich did, and I've had other dreams that turned out to be real events as I dreamed them. Once I had a dream that I was visiting a friend across the street and woke up by his front door, completely disoriented. Another time I dreamed that I was reading poetry. The next morning, I found a book of poems on the table in our family room which hadn't been there before. It was open at the page containing the poem from my dream. I remember dreaming about a birthday party I went to when I was a kid. I told my mom, and she said, 'I didn't know you remembered that. It was a long time ago. You were only four, I think.'

"I believe that dreams and reality can be one and the same thing, at least for me. I even went to a psychiatrist about my dream problem, as I called it, but that didn't help me much. Do you think I should have been a psychiatrist rather than a marine biologist?"

Grandpa's dreams about the truck drivers and the so-called "igloo" cult flashed through Regina's mind. She wondered whether Grandpa's dreams were as vivid as Phil's, or whether he had ever walked in his sleep. He had never mentioned it.

"No, Phil. Science is a good career. You can't do everything," she said, not caring whether he was a scientist or a psychiatrist.

Chapter 26

Regina continued to be bothered by what Grandpa had told the journalist, especially about his youth, which she had never heard before. It seemed at odds with what she knew about him. Was everything he'd told the journalist about his parents true? She would try to check it out on the new and much improved browser, INFO, which was a remarkably reliable source of information.

What she learned shocked her. First, Grandpa's father was an import-export lawyer, not a stockbroker, and he was killed in a car crash when he was sixty-four. Moreover, the crash occurred two years *after* Grandpa had started his job at the Vision Science Center. There was no mention of Grandpa's father ever having ALS. Well, maybe INFO had missed that. In any case, Grandpa apparently did not postpone his career after he received his Ph.D. to care for his father before plunging into work.

However, some things Grandpa said were true according to what she found on INFO. Grandpa's mother, Beatrice, had been an actress, and he was raised in a theatrical environment, so performing was probably stressed, and maybe the line between acting and reality was fuzzy. Regina knew that Grandpa had a flair for fiction and far-out ideas. Perhaps he had been "playacting" for the journalist—not that that would have pardoned him for being untruthful. Far-fetched, but ...

When checking Grandpa's version of the absurd government regulations and low morale of the employees at the Vision Science Center, INFO confirmed what Grandpa had said once, namely that business trips could not be linked in any way with vacation annual leave. She also verified other cumbersome rules Grandpa had mentioned to her and probably to the journalist as well.

"Grandpa wasn't lying to be deceitful," she uttered to the empty room, trying her best to give him credibility.

Regina found that the rules driving Grandpa crazy had been established to make the government appear democratic, above board in every conceivable category, and a model of trustworthiness, but that had had unintended consequences. Good intentions aren't always successful. The government environment may have felt so repressive, so dysfunctional, that he truly believed it could have kindled a rebellious conspiracy, or at least driven a single angry, mentally deranged person to engineer the Obliteration. Mass murders and sabotage have often been the result of a mentally sick person throughout history.

Regina wanted to put all this information into a coherent package: Grandpa was a smart but unreliable narrator. He was raised by a single parent in a theater world, in which stories, performance and entertainment prevailed. But by ninety he was a lonely, old widower with an outsized imagination, and he was bitter that he hadn't been appreciated by his fellow scientists for his major contribution, Thought-Particles. She wondered whether she was writing a novel or solving a crime. Neither, she concluded. She was searching for a way to reconcile Grandpa's conflations of truth and fantasy, and then how that might relate to the Obliteration, if at all. The contradictions were troublesome, yet her intuition teased her that there might be some explanation for Grandpa's unreliable tales.

She would sleep on it, hoping for clarification when she felt fresh in the morning.

Chapter 27

THE NEXT MORNING Regina sat in her room facing her computer's blank screen, with a doughnut and hot coffee on the table. She wanted to find some approach to understanding Grandpa's meandering "recollections." He had often said that even as a scientist, belief was an essential part of creativity. Thus, she thought, he must have believed whatever he said was the truth. So, she needed belief as well. She had often solved puzzles when she was certain they had an answer. That would be her belief, that there was light at the end of the dark tunnel of confusion, without disregarding anything he had said.

"Good luck," she wished herself. She would find a common thread to weave a consistent narrative of Grandpa's scattered memories.

Grandpa recalled the discrete events of his life as being separate and unconnected. But what if his memories were interdependent? His life was not a series of unrelated happenings; it was a continuum. Each action and thought and event must have had something in common to fit into an essential part of the entire story.

She considered Grandpa's recollections—his observations, thoughts, and dreams—as pieces of his life bundled together, synchronizing his heart and brain, as it were, not isolated bits of unrelated facts. What if each recollection was rooted in various proportions of thoughts and feelings and experiences?

"That could be the way Grandpa viewed his world," she muttered, "as complex blends. But blends of what?"

She thought she was on to something. His diverse recollections were part of the totality of his life, just as an arm or leg was a part of his body, or a thought an indivisible part of his brain. His memories, then, might be recalled by a similar process as well. How would that work?

Grandpa said that his father had criticized him for not being a provider for his family. Perhaps Grandpa imagined his father's criticism due to his own sadness and anger that his father had never answered his dream to have a Dad, with an uppercase D—a loving father—as he grew up. And why did it sting Grandpa so much when he said his father called him a dreamer who played at science? Maybe that was also imagined due to his conflict of desperately wanting to be an important scientist, yet uncertain—indeed, scared—he wouldn't succeed. Grandpa's bringing up Thought-Particles when speaking to the journalist, virtually rubbing salt into the still-open wound of not being accepted by his scientific peers, could be another blend of his disappointment and anger, now imagined, with the real tragedy of the Obliteration.

What about Grandpa's claim of getting close to his estranged father, who he said returned home with ALS? It seemed there was not a word of truth in that. But Grandpa wished he had been closer to his father and might have imagined that he did get closer, while it never actually happened. Overlapping realities and imaginations. What if Grandpa's imagination had a significant role in shaping his recollections, which he perceived as true?

Then what about Grandpa's dreams of the Obliteration? Recollections of those too could have been blends of reality of the Obliteration and what he had written in his diary. Again, part real, part imagined, in varying doses.

Whether correct in detail or not, Regina developed what she called a "bundle hypothesis." Yes, she said to herself, feeling a chill of accomplishment run down her spine. Recollections as blends of reality and imagination! But didn't that cast doubt on exactly what reality was? How, then, to account for diverse perceptions? Well, the imagination part would differ for everyone. Of course, she thought. Reality and imagination are each a separate universe—the reality universe and the imagination universe. Perception and memories occupied both universes simultaneously. Grandpa's recollections were mixtures resulting from his inhabiting the reality universe with a dose of his simultaneous presence in the imagination universe. She continued along that line of reasoning and postulated that the relative roles of the two universes were dynamic and must vary with time, previous experiences, and circumstances.

Am I juggling absurd ideas to rescue Grandpa from being an unreliable narrator and even a liar? she asked herself.

"No!" she exclaimed aloud adamantly, as if she was debating an opponent.

That's when her authoritative inner voice said the following: I'm contributing a new physics of perception that is analogous to that of white light. Understanding Grandpa's recollections requires a "thought prism," as it were, analogous to a prism that resolves white light into different colors in the visible spectrum based on their different wavelengths, as Isaac Newton demonstrated long ago. Each of Grandpa's events and memories and dreams is a bundle that can be resolved by a thought prism into its origins partially in the reality universe and partially in the imagination universe.

There it is, she said to herself proudly: perceptions and recollections comprise an overlap of the reality and imagination universes. A writer might put it another way. Perceptions and recollections stand on two legs—one in the reality universe, the other in the imagination universe—that move in one direction or another, depending on circumstances.

She speculated that Grandpa sensed the world in his own mixture of reality and imagination—a combination of two separate, interacting universes—which made his perceptions and memories—indeed, his reality—unique for him alone, not lies. Another person with similar experiences would perceive the world differently, mainly because their reality would be mixed with a different quantity and quality of imagination.

"Yes," Regina said under her breath, "each person's reality inhabits the imagination universe comprised of personal imponderables."

Okay, she thought, imagining that this might become a short story, what's my insight in a nutshell?

The answer fell into place as if dropped from the heavens. It boiled down to the imagination universe, which had always been in plain sight, but never recognized as an integral component that affected each person's perception and reality. The two universes—reality and imagination—were continually interacting with each other. Neither existed without the other, because there always was and always will be that which is known reality and that which is imagined, and, most mysterious, that which is not yet known to exist.

Regina had finally discovered, thanks to Grandpa as her experimental subject, a new universe by re-interpreting and expanding what was always lingering in the background—imagination. She recognized its essential role for perceptions, recollections, and personal reality.

She wished she could share her discovery, but with whom? Alone, she shed the happiest tears since the day she was accepted at Caltech.

Chapter 28

REGINA, FEELING AT peace, imagined herself amid lush vegetation with birds chirping. She closed her eyes to float in the moment. Suddenly, she heard breathing and feet shuffling. The atmosphere had changed from calm to a restless energy she couldn't identify.

She opened her eyes and there stood Grandpa with another man. But Grandpa was dead; how could he be in front of her looking very much alive?

"I can't believe this. Grandpa, is that you? Are you alive? Am I dead? Who's with you? Is he alive or dead?"

She answered herself. "Of course, he must be Ricardo, your other half, so to speak. Am I right? Am I looking at two dead men?"

"Oh, sweetie, I can't believe how good it is to see you again," said Grandpa. "Yes, I'm dead, you know that. Dead people have their own reality and can stay alive in the minds of others. Do you know how that happens? I have a theory: it's by Thought-Particles! Those elusive little devils transfer vertically as well as horizontally. That must be it. I can't wait until someone isolates a Thought-Particle. Who knows, that might be you. Wouldn't that be great? I'm sure that of all the innovations and discoveries that have been made throughout history, Thought-Particles—*my* Thought-Particles—will turn out to have the greatest impact. Sorry, I'm rambling and tooting my own horn. And yes again, this is Ricardo."

Ricardo waved to Regina but didn't say anything.

Regina let a minute pass in silence, which she felt as an eternity of confusion and awe.

Grandpa looked happy and rested. He was thriving as a dead man. He started to speak, but before he could say anything, Ricardo, a rather short, slightly obese, balding, messily dressed fellow wearing bright orange socks, took the helm.

"Regina, dear ..."

"Please, don't call me dear," she interrupted, thinking of Mom. "My name is Regina."

"Okay, no problem, Regina," he said without a trace of appearing rejected. "I'm excited to meet you, the most recent addition to our genetic lineage."

There they were—Ricardo and Grandpa—standing before her. What had made them come? Did they sense that I wanted to share my discovery with someone? No, that couldn't be it.

"Let's not beat around the bush, Regina," said Grandpa. "Ricardo and I know your thoughts about imagination being a universe. Dead people know what's going on. You'll understand when you join us, but that's a long way off. Anyway, I want to say ..."

"No, no, Roger, let me say it," Ricardo piped up. "I'm the senior person here, at least by age. I want to be the first to tell her."

Grandpa scratched his thighs and shook his head but acquiesced, as he usually did. "Okay. You're being self-centered, Ricardo, as always. It doesn't matter. Truth prevails in the long run no matter who says it." He paused. "Unless it doesn't, or there is no truth."

Grandpa hasn't changed a bit, she thought, still stretching every thought into endless possibilities. She was so happy to see him again.

"I don't care who says it, whatever 'it' is. Just tell me!" said Regina, becoming more comfortable in this extraordinary company. They were family, after all.

"No one, not even dead people, know exactly what will happen in the future," Grandpa said, as if cautioning her. "We're not prophets or fortune tellers, and we do make mistakes, although infrequently, I'd say."

"Quit being self-centered, Roger," Ricardo said.

"All right. You've got the floor, Ricardo. Tell Regina whatever you want," he said, scratching his thighs.

"Thanks, Roger. Finally." He turned to Regina and said, "I don't know if you fully realize the importance of what you've discovered. You will go down in history. That was the 'it' we wanted to tell you. Your expansion of imagination into a universe that contributes to and overlaps perception of reality and memories is a far-reaching concept, as significant, maybe even more so, than jellyfish seeing evolution or Thought-Particles. You've leaped into a league of your own."

She shook her head self-consciously, yet deep inside, she knew it.

"Go ahead and tell her more, Ricardo."

"Yes, sure. I know, Roger," said Ricardo. "Anyway, Regina, before going into the implications of an imagination universe—and there are many—I want to make sure I understand what you mean. I want us to be on the same wavelength."

Regina nodded. "Sure. What are your thoughts about the imagination universe?"

"Okay. You have shown that each of our perceptions and memories comprises our past bundled with the present. Yes? Correct? Whatever we perceive or remember is a complex mixture of our real experiences and observations with imagination, which is never at rest. Our memories blur because the part that is imagination—the part that 'wobbles,' as it were—hops around in its universe. I love your analogy of resolving your so-called 'bundle' with a thought-prism, as Sir Isaac Newton— what a smart fellow he was—resolved white light into an array of colors with different wavelengths. Brilliant analogy! It puts abstract imagination in the realm of physics, a new mental physics. What a supportive granddaughter you are, putting imagination in the realm of a new physics, as Roger—Grandpa to you—put abstract thoughts in the form of particles. I'd say both are a triumph of imagination."

Grandpa's face lit up. He rubbed his thighs again, this time more like caresses than nervous scratches. He looked happy to be recognized, if only by his best friend.

"My hearty congratulations, Regina," continued Ricardo. "You've created the physics of imagination. Do you realize how important that is? New concepts are truly creative."

Regina nodded. "I sort of did. But I thought that my concept might be a derivative of Sigmund Freud from way, way back in the twentieth century, when he said that the unconscious mind drives us to repeat ourselves without realizing that the thoughts and emotions from the past influence the present. It's kind of expanding déjà vu, wouldn't you say?" she said with modesty. "Didn't Freud mean that behavior encompasses a bundle of past experiences, in so many words? Proust too, with his madeleines and déjà vu. The twentieth century was certainly productive! Probably I'm wandering into areas I don't understand. It's a bad habit. Nevertheless, I'm excited about seeing imagination as a universe—our interior universe—that works in cahoots with the exterior reality, and that our view of the world and our memories exist as a combination of the two universes working together. How it all works, and to what extent it occurs in animals, and how the imagination universe evolved, those are the questions to pursue, not who said what first."

"That's great, Queen Regina," Grandpa said. He let it go at that, for when something was right, it didn't need further explanation. It was just right.

Ricardo was clapping and almost dancing with excitement. "Yes, yes, Regina. What great questions! And you're so modest."

What an enthusiastic guy, she thought, trying to stay calm, though she was excited and proud and more convinced than ever about her imagination universe. If both Grandpa and Ricardo thought it was right, what more did she need? It must be right.

Ricardo carried on as a self-appointed lecturer. He loved to talk and hadn't had a captive audience in a long time. He said that people must have inhabited the imagination universe from the beginning of recorded history, and no doubt way before that as well. He bet that most animals roamed in some form of the imagination universe, even jellyfish with their diffuse brains. Imagination! He loved it!

"Whatever we imagine is a mere speck in its universe," he said. "Imagination can't escape its universe. Imagination is like a person, who is a singular body of flesh and blood, but more so as well. A person always includes thoughts and possessions and ancestry and friends as well as enemies. See what I mean? A person is a universe, and much more than a singular being who breathes, eats, sleeps, and dies."

Ricardo paused for a moment before continuing. "But there is a major difference between a person and imagination," he said. "Imagination is immortal. It never dies, whatever strange route it takes. It remains in its universe for others to find. Oh my. Imagination is the heart of creativity, it's a driving force like an engine that's always on—like perpetual energy with limitless fuel, but it never escapes its universe."

Ricardo stopped again to take a breath.

"Thoughts, on the other hand, are singular abstractions that stand by themselves, while imagination infiltrates and modifies the whole … the whole shebang!"

He continued, saying that great discoveries are often first imagined, until they became facts in one form or other.

Grandpa listened quietly, nodding his agreement as if he knew all that.

Regina thought that Ricardo was exaggerating and getting trite, but what did she know about how dead people think? Did they imagine new things, or were they limited to their past or sensing what living people thought and imagined? She wasn't in a hurry to find out what dead people are like; she was willing to wait.

"Are you trying to justify your work that others didn't take seriously?" said Roger, speaking directly to Ricardo, as he had done in the past when Ricardo was an inseparable apparition in his mind.

"I'm talking about the work of both of us—you and me," Ricardo said. "Remember, Roger, scientists didn't exactly get wild with excitement about Thought-Particles. But Regina, she's a different story."

"How's that?"

Regina took a step back, realizing that she wasn't in the conversation anymore. Ricardo and Grandpa were discussing as two scientists interacting and sounding as one voice.

She listened.

"Imagination played a key role in my research on jellyfish," Ricardo said. "No one would speculate that jellyfish have a brain of sorts and could visualize evolution based on what was known at the time, or even now. That speculation required imagination, whatever the truth turns out to be. And having that imagination ... hmmmm ... got me into trouble, but in retrospect, considering Regina's speculations, maybe my imagination was special. My imagined world won't die with me. It will remain in its universe. It's not dead, like I am. See what I mean? Imagination is a whole universe, as she says! Once that's appreciated, everything looks different."

"Are you sorry that you leaped to your jellyfish speculations when you did, Ricardo?" Roger asked.

"Absolutely not. Think about it."

Ricardo suddenly put on his professional mask and used his professorial voice. He dived into the essence of his research since his audience was two other scientists. "The idea that any animal, even jellyfish, can see evolution wasn't far off the mark, even then. Doesn't the genome— the DNA—of each species have remnants of their ancestors? Don't their successors carry those genes along with their evolution? You know they do. Evolution can be traced by genetic sequencing of multiple species. What's missing is proof that jellyfish, or any animal, can *see* evolution by having genetic information expressed as a visual image in a kind of 'mind's eye,' or in some other form that we still don't know.

"We need a little modesty, like I see in Regina. We understand one aspect of genetic expression—DNA makes RNA which makes protein. DNA and RNA have other functions but never mind that for now. Fine. But it took a long time to learn the genetic code and the protein synthesis role for DNA. What if DNA has additional roles as well, roles that are expressed by different properties, say energy differences among the nucleotides affected by context? We need to be patient. New forms of DNA expression and functions will show up, at least that's my bet. Now that I think about it, perhaps all that's needed is to discover how proteins directed by inherited ancient DNA could create a mechanism for visualizing evolution represented in their genes. I'm not at all sorry I brought all that up, because I felt then, and still do now, that it's probably true in some fashion, and I'm proud that I envisioned it first. I'd better stop there before I say anything stupid. Maybe I have already.

But stupidity, whatever that is, is certainly an unexpected part of the imagination universe."

Ricardo gazed out as if he was looking within himself, both pleased and haunted. Regina sensed he worried that he spoke too much—perhaps he was feeling vulnerable, she thought. But he spoke his heart and seemed sincere, she was sure about that. He clearly wished he could continue his research to prove himself correct, to roam some more in the imagination universe. He was dead, she knew that, but still curious and ambitious. Now it was her turn to continue, to credit him and Grandpa for their contributions, which she thought were significant.

Regina took note of every word and asked, "So, Ricardo, you've described a potential mechanism—fantasy at this stage—that might prove your speculation about jellyfish seeing evolution. Any more ideas?"

"You're persistent, aren't you. Relentless is more like it. It's a good trait, even if it may bury you at the end."

Before Ricardo had time to continue speculating, Roger chipped in. "Tell us more about imagination in science. What about Thought-Particles? Can you tie that in somehow?"

Ricardo appeared anxious to respond. "My point, lady and gentleman, is what Regina has clarified to some extent: imagination is not trivial, it's a great accomplishment, even if it precedes proof. Proof is another dimension of discovery, a different achievement altogether, a milestone. However, proof is separate from imagination. I have imagined visualizing evolution, with sound reasoning, if I say so myself. You, Roger, have imagined abstract thoughts carried on infectious particles, also advanced on credible observations. The infectious nature of Thought-Particles is a brilliant idea, since it implies that we get some of our thoughts from other people passively without realizing it. It makes us all partly everyone else. You've said that in your article, and that's supposed to be nothing? Nonsense. It's something important. The idea alone is a major contribution. It's independent of proof. Eventually proof may turn out in some cases to be no more than a technical contribution, not a conceptual one."

Grandpa nodded and appeared happy with what Ricardo was

saying. He looked at Regina and smiled. She returned his smile. Her crooked tooth didn't bother her.

"Our hypotheses—seeing evolution, thoughts as particles—both imagination—opened new arenas to enter, new ways of thinking about nature in multiple perspectives, such as Rabbi what's-his-name, oh yes, Rabbi Magnum, picking up on Thought-Particles in a religious context," Ricardo continued. "Imagination plays a big part in science that both precedes and succeeds discovery, and it should be recognized as such. Proved or not, imaginations by themselves can be important contributions to science. Congratulations to both of us!"

"Don't take credit for Regina's contribution, Ricardo. *She* discovered the significance of the imagination universe, not you or me."

Ricardo looked chagrined and muttered, "Sorry, Regina. Congratulations to the *three* of us."

Roger extended what Ricardo brought up. "Imagination ignites creative sparks, as you say. We've been short-changed. Regina will resurrect our reputations, won't you?"

She suddenly felt insecure. "I'll try," she said, although she had no notion of how she would do that.

"First," she continued, "I've another implication of the imagination universe that both of you have missed.

They sat up. "What's that?" asked Grandpa.

"The imagination universe is more than a world for us to inhabit."

Ricardo and Roger were straining to hear more, as if she was about to drop another gem.

"I propose that imagination is one of our senses, like vision or hearing or taste and so on. I bet we have 'imagination receptors,' like each sense has its extensive set of specific receptors. Color-blind, or partially blind, or totally blind individuals each sense the world differently. Ditto for hearing, or for preferences in foods, and so on. The senses depend on separate receptors, which vary in quality and intensity, as does imagination."

Ricardo and Grandpa were speechless, creating an awe of respect, such as a silent pause immediately following a great performance of music or theater that precedes the applause and
a standing ovation.

Regina went on. "Perhaps we can consider imagination an illegal alien of reality, until it becomes legal—in other words, real. Yes, I like that," she added, as if talking to herself. "Imagination as an alien citizen of the real world, worthy of recognition. I think it's going to take more time for the cause of the Obliteration to move from the imagination universe to the reality universe. Maybe it will never happen. Not every alien becomes legal, not everything imagined becomes real."

"I like the way you put that," said Grandpa. "A benefit of being dead is that time is eternal. I can wait as long as it takes for Thought-Particles to switch from an alien to an accepted reality."

"What do you think about that, Ricardo?" Regina asked. "Can you wait indefinitely for proof that jellyfish see evolution?"

"Indefinitely is no longer than right now for a dead person," Ricardo said. "So, sure, no rush to be where I am already."

"Same here," Grandpa said. "I'm at my destination, the place I imagined when I was alive, waiting for everyone else to arrive. It's relaxing not having to rush."

"Love it!" Regina said. "But I'm not waiting for anyone to arrive, and I don't have endless time."

"Not yet, Regina. You're young," Ricardo added. "You can't appreciate the time dimensions of imagination and discovery yet. My speculations on jellyfish seeing evolution and Roger's on Thought-Particles may take another century or two to be realized—if they're ever proved at all. It's not long for us. We'll wait."

"Right on, Ricardo," said Grandpa, cheerfully.

What a treat, Regina thought, to be present at the source of great discoveries of the imagination before anyone knows how important these ideas are, and that they might become real with time. Hurray for imagination, an indispensable—and independent—resource for science, which, on occasion, is tethered to truth.

"Proof is a straggler behind imagination, right?" Regina asked rhetorically.

Ricardo nodded but wasn't satisfied. "Enough," he interrupted. "I still want to know what's practical about the imagination universe. How does it affect our everyday life apart from our perceptions?" He looked at Regina for an answer.

She was still as a statue, her heart beating so strongly she feared it might burst out of her chest. What did they want her to say? How imagination was practical? Goodness, what to say? Perhaps it was a trap and Ricardo was testing whether she really understood the significance of the imagination universe. She squinted, as if that would help her to know what to say, but her mind was blank, and she was scared to look like a stupid, silly little girl with a big mouth.

Her left eyelid fluttered. Grandpa scratched his thighs, and she looked at Ricardo's orange socks, the ones Grandpa had told her he wore only on major events. What to tell these two smart scientists, her relatives, who never received the credit they deserved? What to say? What to say? she repeated to herself for emphasis. She wanted a hint, and then Grandpa gave her a cryptic one, as if he had just received a Thought-Particle from her asking for assistance.

"Don't you sometimes feel like an astronaut in the vacuum, drifting between two galaxies, one filled with stars and the other empty, and you don't know which one to explore? Does the empty one draw you in it for some reason? Why?" Grandpa said, and then he raised his eyebrows as if signaling that he was trying to help her.

Ricardo mumbled, "That's how I felt when I was in La Parguera collecting jellyfish. Between paradise and reality, I chose paradise, but then suffered the reality."

"Regina, what are your practical thoughts about imagination?" Grandpa continued, as if Ricardo hadn't interrupted him. "For example, our senses that you brought up—seeing, hearing, feeling—determine our practical existence. We don't bump into things that we see are in our path. We eat what tastes good. We listen to music we like. Tell us more about your idea of imagination as a daily sense.

"Ricardo and I didn't take the trouble to come here only to leave without having received all your wisdom. You're young, not spoiled yet by life's pressures, not limited by the thoughts and bias of others. Tell us how the imagination universe, or imagination 'sense,' as you speculate, affects our everyday reality, as the other senses do."

Regina didn't know what to say, until she did. She often developed her ideas by speaking, sometimes to herself, usually to others. The adage, "necessity is the mother of invention," worked for her, and at this moment it was a necessity to tell them the role of the imagination universe in everyday life. She was a storyteller, a writer at heart, a creative person who imagined. What should she tell her insistent relatives about imagination being a practical sense?

A story, of course.

Chapter 29

R EGINA STARTED HER story without knowing how to finish it. She would make it up—use her imagination—as she talked. As often happened, she became so involved in her fictional tale, laced with truth and infiltrated with imagination, that she made small detours along the way that weren't relevant to the main message. These digressions enriched the story for her, just as imagination enriched her life. Detours were about imagination. Sometimes when she spun a yarn, as she was about to do, she would laugh because she thought the story was funny enough to be true; sometimes her eyes would moisten because she knew that even if the story was fiction, a similar sad truth existed somewhere else.

She told them a story that she made up on the spot.

Ruggles

A middle-aged man had just learned that he had been rejected by his law firm to become a partner. He had to find a new job. Apart from being distraught and ashamed, he was the breadwinner and was scared to tell his wife and daughter. How would they react?

He had to "digest" his unfortunate situation, so he told his wife that he needed to go on an overnight business trip and would be back the next day. This was not unusual, so she accepted it without comment. Then he went to a hotel in town for the night.

Despondent, wishing he were dead, he flipped on the television and caught the news. The top story of the day was a policeman who had mistaken a man walking his Great Dane, Ruggles, for a prowler. Apparently Ruggles, a strong dog, had pulled the leash out of his master's hand in a classy residential neighborhood and was sniffing around a flower bed in front of a home with a child's tricycle on the driveway next to a basketball hoop. The net was set low, consistent with at least one very young child living there. The dog's owner, a chef in a local restaurant, had immigrated from Lithuania ten years ago. He was approximately thirty years old, wore a jogging outfit, and was unarmed. He was shot and killed crossing the front lawn to retrieve his dog.

"I'm so sorry," said the policeman to the press after he shot the man. "My mistake."

"Is that sufficient—to be sorry?" asked the newsman questioning the policeman.

"No, but what can I do? Stuff happens. It is what it is. I meant well. Reality can be hard to accept sometimes. And if the gentleman had been a murderer well, wouldn't that make me a hero? I imagined he was a murderer."

The man watching television was too discouraged with his own problems to take someone else's tragedy seriously. Shootings, deadly accidents, and indifference to human life were common throughout history. Racism—black, brown, yellow—cast its ugly spell for generations.

The discouraged man muttered, "A fair and peaceful world is impossible to imagine."

The news report segued from the killing of the Lithuanian to his Great Dane, Ruggles. What would happen to Ruggles now that his master was dead?

That was the idea Regina was looking for. She could now conclude the story.

> *Yes, Ruggles. He needed a home. Did he have all his vaccinations so he wouldn't spread disease? Many dog owners refused to vaccinate their pets as a matter of principle. A surprising number of owners believed that they owned their pets, not the government, and their decision was best for their pets. It was a free country! They were ready to take it to the Supreme Court, especially since seven of the nine justices were dog owners. Of the other two justices, one had a cat, and the ninth was progressive with tropical fish. Even fish, he thought, provided company; all it took was some imagination. Always imagination—why kill anyone, where would Ruggles go, when is choice free or mandatory, are fish company or decoration or obligations to feed? Imagination was the foundation that made anything possible, perhaps even determining what was right or wrong. Imagination ruled in its vast universe.*

Regina interrupted her story to apologize for digressing from the main points now and then, cryptic as it might sound. She got carried away. She continued:

> *The news commentator continued to talk about Ruggles. Why had he pulled away from his owner—was he being mistreated? One could only imagine. But Ruggles apparently had a mind of his own. What was the dog thinking? More space for imagination.*
>
> *The discouraged man imagined that a kind foster home would be found for Ruggles, hopefully one that would give comfort to a lonely animal. How reassuring imagination could be, to wring drops of benefit from the flood of tragedy, perhaps even comfort to someone fired from a coveted job.*
>
> *Ruggles's dark, soulful eyes made the unfortunate death of his master extra sad. Imagining the dog's distress took attention away from the man's death. Each—the dog and the man, separate entities—affected the other. Poor Ruggles. So sad. He needed a home.*

The despondent man closed his eyes and imagined Ruggles lying next to him, comforting him, facilitating peace. As sleep caressed him, he dreamed of being swallowed by quicksand—soft, slippery mud that crept up his legs and body. The sensation was so vivid that he gasped for breath in his sleep, as if his dream was real. He could sense the mud. When the mud reached his neck, he gasped again, then felt calm as he submerged completely into it. Death in the dream had won the battle. Like the Lithuanian's, his life was over. There was nothing left to worry about. The dream was gone. He experienced "nothingness" in his sleep.

When the man awoke in the morning, he thought—imagined—that he was dead, as he had felt himself die peacefully when the quicksand swallowed him. To convince himself that his dream wasn't reality, he pinched himself and bit his lip. "Ouch!" he exclaimed when he drew blood from his lower lip. He drank a glass of water, which felt cool in his mouth, and he was finally convinced that he was alive. The reality was that he didn't have Ruggles, and he wasn't a Lithuanian. He was an American without a dog who had been rejected as partner in his law firm. But his imagination had given him Ruggles, which allowed him to sleep, and his dream—more imagination—made him appreciate the reality that he was alive. These gifts were preferable to the death in his dream. The dream was just a dream, not reality. Yet Ruggles was reality. Imagination taught him that rejection from a law firm wasn't as final as death.

Dreams, reality. True, false. So many choices to make by using imagination. Sometimes dreams and reality weren't that different from one another, and sometimes they needed each other to clarify what was imagined and what was real. Sometimes they were opposites. Reality and imagination, including dreams, were in different universes which overlapped in constantly changing ways. The trick was to tease them apart, just as a prism resolves white light.

Regina had surprised herself as she unraveled the layers of her story. Having convinced herself that she did have something to offer mankind, she stopped to let her words sink in. It was deathly quiet in the room.

Finally, she stood tall and said, "Imagination is bigger than a component of creativity, much bigger; it's a universe and a sense. It can be as difficult to recognize as it can be to isolate truth from falsehood, and as impossible to escape from as a black hole. We all inhabit the imagination universe as well as the reality universe. We flip back and forth between these two worlds—the personal one, imagination, and the external one, reality. We often don't know which universe we're in because we exist in a dynamic blend of both. Together, they give us our fragile perceptions and realities.

"Imagine! We're not sentenced to a single universe. Our lives have more space and are more interesting and complex than they would be if they were limited to one, external universe. And what does that mean in terms of our awareness of what's true or not? It means that there isn't an absolute answer, just like the Obliteration doesn't have a known cause—yet—because it's still in the imagination universe. Oh, my, it's exhausting and extraordinary."

Regina had told her story with her eyes closed, for everything she said was an expression of what was inside her. That's where she looked, inside herself, where her imagination universe resided.

After a short pause, she had one more message, the one she deemed most important of all, the accomplishment of her mission that freed her to be Queen Regina.

"I am proud to follow Roger Resin—Grandpa—and Ricardo Sztein, both pioneers and visionaries, in inhabiting the imagination universe as a driving force in basic research. It opens new vistas that may have been set aside or rejected because, at first glance, they seem too formidable or unfathomable.

"What fits comfortably in the reality universe is valuable, of course, we all know that, but the ideas and insights that roam in the imagination universe have the power to change our view of the world, to affect our concept of reality. We exist in the complex, twin universes—not separate fraternal twins, but Siamese twins of reality and imagination—each separate yet interconnected and mutually dependent on each other.

"Ricardo and Grandpa," she said, seeing their faces in her mind with her eyes still closed, "will forever be recognized for providing the foundation for the importance of the imagination universe, which I believe may be our salvation from a world that is fraught with frightening and dangerous elements."

She had nothing more to add. When she opened her eyes, Ricardo and Grandpa were nowhere in sight.

Had they ever been there?

Maybe.

Probably, she thought. It didn't matter anymore.

Also in the
Jellyfish Have Eyes Series

Jellyfish Have Eyes

BENEATH THE WATERS in the hidden world of the mangrove swamps of La Parguera, Puerto Rico, lurks the mysterious jellyfish.

Government researcher Ricardo Sztein is obsessed with unlocking its secrets.

Ignoring his wife's dying warning, "be careful", he risks everything to peer into the remarkable world of jellyfish vision.

But in a cutthroat lab where careers are made or broken, can he afford to follow his curiosity?

Roger's Thought-Particles

WHAT IF YOUR thoughts weren't entirely your own?

Dr. Roger Resin, an ambitious scientist and visionary, has a radical hypothesis: What if thoughts could be transmitted through infectious particles? His peers scoff at the idea, dismissing it as pure fantasy. But when his research attracts attention from an unexpected source, Roger is thrust into a whirlwind of intrigue, doubt, and discovery.

As he delves deeper, Roger must confront the fine line between genius and madness, science and speculation, truth and destiny. Will his groundbreaking idea revolutionize the way we understand the human mind, or will it cost him everything?

Written by a renowned scientist, Roger's Thought-Particles is a gripping, thought-provoking novel that explores the thrilling highs and crushing lows of scientific discovery. Perfect for fans of speculative fiction and scientific thrillers, this book will leave you questioning where your thoughts truly come from.

Are you ready to rethink reality?

Acknowledgments

I AM GRATEFUL to Barbara Esstman and Lucy Chumbley for their invaluable editorial comments and expert editing, which have improved this novel greatly. I am also grateful to the excellent and meticulous copy editing of David Bamford. I thank Margaret Dimond for her incisive and helpful comments and management of Truth and Fantasy Media LLC. I thank Ismael Carrillo, an award designer, for his superb cover illustration. Finally, a big thank you to Lona, my wife, for her love and patience.

About the Author

J ORAM PIATIGORSKY, PRESENTLY an emeritus scientist at the National Institutes of Health, writes fiction, memoir, and essays and blogs on his website (www.joramp.com) and Substack (jorampiatigorsky.substack.com). He has won numerous science awards and trained a generation of scientists. He collects Inuit art (www.inuitbeautiful.com) and lives in Bethesda with his wife, Lona. They have two sons and five grandchildren. He loves to hear from readers, and can be reached at jorampiatigorsky@gmail.com.

www.ingramcontent.com/pod-product-compliance
Lightning Source LLC
Chambersburg PA
CBHW022124170626
46808CB00002B/831